Ballerina Stories

Chosen by Emma Young

Illustrated by Lara Jones

MACMILLAN CHILDREN'S BOOKS

Pour Mamie. E. Y.

To Bethy Bee and Ray-Ray. L. J.

First published 2007 by Macmillan Children's Books
a division of Macmillan Publishers Limited
20 New Wharf Road, London N1 9RR
Basingstoke and Oxford
Associated companies throughout the world
www.panmacmillan.com

ISBN 978-0-330-45273-1

This collection copyright © Macmillan Children's Books 2007
Stories copyright © Ian Billings, Jan Burchett, Geraldine McCaughrean,
Julia Donaldson, Fiona Dunbar, Belinda Hollyer, Bel Mooney,
Vic Parker, Sara Vogler and Anna Wilson
Illustrations copyright © Lara Jones 2007

The acknowledgements on page 341 constitute an
extension to this copyright page.

The right of Lara Jones to be identified as the
illustrator of this work has been asserted by her in accordance
with the Copyright, Designs and Patents Act 1988.

3 5 7 9 8 6 4

A CIP catalogue record for this book is available from
the British Library.

Typset by Nigel Hazle
Printed and bound in the UK by CPI Mackays, Chatham, ME5 8TD

Contents

The Nutcracker

Geraldine McCaughrean

Once upon a time there was a perfect Christmas. Oh, it did not start very well, but for Clara Stahlbaum it was to be the Christmas she would remember for the rest of her life, and describe to her own children as if it were a fairy tale — which indeed it was, in a way.

Christmas was always magical in the Stahlbaum house. Clara and Fritz looked forward to it for weeks beforehand, talked of nothing else. On Christmas Eve they peeped down through the banisters to see ladies arriving in velvet dresses and fur muffs, men carrying tall hats dusty with snow — and lots of children too excited to behave nicely. Clara and Fritz ran downstairs to greet their friends and to be ready, there — right there on the threshold – when the doors of the dining room were opened.

All day the doors had been locked, sealing secrets of Christmas. With a flood of light that spilled out into the hall, they swung open now. Why, it hardly looked like the dining room at all, but some magical garden, the tree spangled with candles, the wineglasses glittering like ice on the snow-white tablecloth, the flowers filling every alcove, mantelpiece and sill. Piled around the base of the tree was

3

a mountain of presents in bright wrappings. And there, at the top of the tree, her wand outstretched as if she had just decorated the room by magic, balanced the Christmas Fairy, her head made of a sugarplum and her dress out of spun sugar.

For Clara there was a dress and a cot for her dolls, a sugar cane – and one gift she had wanted more than anything in the world: a pair of pink ballet shoes so beautiful they made her eyes gleam with tears.

4

Naturally, Clara started dancing.

Suddenly, just as the clock in the hall struck nine, all the candles guttered in a fierce, cold draught that made everybody shudder. For a moment the room was almost dark. Something black brushed past Mama Stahlbaum and she gave a little shriek. Then the candles flared up again and there stood a tall, thin old man all in black, his face hidden by a huge snow-sodden hood, a black sack at his feet. There was a dreadful silence.

5

'Drossy!' cried Clara. 'It's Uncle Drosselmeyer!' And she ran and hugged the old man. 'I wasn't frightened one bit!'

'Drosselmeyer, you old rogue!' bellowed Papa Stahlbaum. 'How you do like to cause a stir!' But everyone was delighted to see the old Professor. No Christmas was quite complete without him – or his famous presents.

No toyshop in the world ever sold toys as splendid as the toys the Professor made. This Christmas Eve, however, Professor Drosselmeyer had brought more than presents to the party.

'Let me introduce you to my nephew, Karl.'

'Never mind him,' said Fritz. 'What have you brought me?'

'I'm very pleased to meet you, Karl,' said Clara, and curtsied to the young man. What a handsome boy! What a gentle smile. Why can't Fritz be more like him? Clara found herself thinking.

'Well then, let's see . . .' Uncle

Drossy sank his beaky nose into the deep, black sack. 'For my godchildren I have this year a clockwork mouse . . .'

'I'll have that!' cried Fritz and snatched it.

'A hobby horse to *share*,' said Drosselmeyer sternly.

'Oh, *I'll* have that!' cried Fritz and, throwing the mouse aside, snatched up the hobby horse.

'A box of toy soldiers . . .'

The hobby horse was flung down and Fritz scattered all the soldiers about – beautiful models painted with scarlet uniforms, cockaded hats, glossy boots and bandoleers with buckles of gold.

'But this is just for my little Clara,' said Drossy. 'Miss Clara – meet Captain Kracko!' He laid the toy in her arms: another soldier but much bigger than the others and carved of wood. His head was enormous, with a gigantic set of white teeth fixed in a big grin. The black flaps of his jacket lifted up, and as they did so Captain Kracko's mouth dropped open. 'Well? He's hungry. Won't you offer the poor gentleman a nut to eat?' suggested Drossy. Clara popped in a little hazelnut and, with a snap of his coat tails, and a smack of his hips, Captain Kracko shelled the nut.

'A nutcracker! Just what I need!' shouted Fritz, tearing across the room.

'No, no! This is Clara's special toy,' said Uncle Drossy firmly.

'*Hers?* A soldier for a girl?' Fritz was so put out that he snatched the nutcracker anyway and forced

a huge walnut between its jaws.
Then, when he could not make the
crackers close, he smashed its gaping
head against the floor.

Clara burst into such tears that
Christmas itself might have lain
there on the floor, broken past
repair.

Karl Drosselmeyer did what he
could. He bandaged the wounded
soldier with a giant pocket
handkerchief, and Clara laid him
in her new doll's crib. Uncle Drossy
called for dancing, and the little

tragedy seemed forgotten as the waltzes began. But Clara did not forget, could not forget. Even after the guests had said goodnight, the candles had gone out, the family had climbed to their beds and the big house had fallen quiet, Clara could not put the wounded Captain out of her mind. She had to creep downstairs and see if his poor head was truly broken past mending.

It was midnight. Uncle Drossy's eerie clock was just striking the hour as she entered the dining room. The

12

great tree loomed darkly in front
of the window. A smouldering log
rolled in the grate. Clara tucked
up Captain Kracko in his little bed
and kissed his big lopsided mouth.
'Poor dear,' she yawned, exhausted.
'I love you anyway, broken or not.'
The tree rustled its branches.

And then another noise! A sudden
movement by the skirting board. A
scuttering of claws. Clara leaped
on to the great sofa and drew her
nightdress tight round her feet. A
mouse!

Scared of a little mouse? You would have been too if you had seen it. For it was *huge* – bigger than a rat, bigger than a cat, bigger than a dog – bigger, when it had finished growing, than Clara herself. In one crooked claw it held a sabre, and between its tattered ears balanced a golden crown. 'Advance, mice, and kill the enemy while he's sleeping!' rasped the Mouse King.

'Sleeping? That's what you think!' cried a fearless voice, and Captain Kracko leaped to his feet.

14

Was it him? Could it be? He seemed so much taller, almost of a height with the Mouse King. And the toy soldiers who sprang to arms at his rallying cry were at least as tall as Clara.

The mice charged. The troopers fixed silver bayonets to their rifles and launched a counter strike. Blood-curdling war cries from the Mouse King mingled with stirring shouts from the Captain. Clara curled down among the cushions at first, but the fight became so

thrilling that she knelt up and beat
with her fists on the sofa back:
'Come on, soldiers! You can trounce
them! *Oh no!*'

An unlucky slip sent the Captain
sprawling, and the Mouse King
was on him in an instant with
slashing sabre cuts that knocked
the Captain's sword from his hand.
There was no time to lose. Clara
pulled off her slipper and threw
it – whack! – at the back of that
mousey head.

The whiskers twitched. The

clawed feet staggered this way
and that. The golden crown went
rolling. Captain Kracko jumped
to his feet and his troopers rallied
round him. They drove the mice off
in one last fearsome attack, which
sent the cowards squealing and
squeaking back to their underground
kingdom to lick their wounds.

'You have saved the day, lady!'
cried the Captain, still breathless as
he saluted her and bowed smartly.
With a click of his heels he said,
'Permit me to crown you with the

captured crown of the Mouse King,
and to escort you to the Queen,
that she may thank you in person
for your bravery!'

'The *Queen*?' gasped Clara.

'Naturally. My mother, the
Queen of my country. Across the
Lemonade Ocean. In the Land of
Sweets.'

She stared at the Captain and,
all at once, realized that he was
not simply a pair of nutcrackers,
not even just a handsome soldier,
but a prince. Oddly, he bore a

strong likeness to old Drosselmeyer's nephew Karl. The two could almost have been brothers.

Off they set, in a huge hollow walnut shell with sails of green angelica and a crew of scarlet-coated soldiers. The Lemonade Ocean fizzed beneath the prow, and a wake of silver bubbles stretched out behind.

All trace of Clara's house was hidden by a sudden swirl of snowflakes. Festivities were already in hand in the Kingdom of Sweets,

to celebrate the great victory over the mice. Bunting hung in the streets and the crowds waving flags lined the waterfront as the walnut-shell boat came into harbour. As Clara stepped ashore, a little gingerbread boy presented her with a bouquet of icing-sugar flowers and hundreds of thousands of hundreds-and-

thousands showered down from
the open windows of every house.
On a green marzipan lawn, under
a meringue canopy, a delicious
banquet of sweets had been laid
along a white-clothed table. Many
coffers of the state treasury had been
emptied of their golden chocolate
coins to pay for the celebrations.

Someone very special was waiting
to lead Clara and the Prince before
the Queen: it was the Sugarplum
Fairy – tall, beautiful, willowy and
dressed in a gown more glistening

21

than liquid sugar. 'Now don't be shy,' she told Clara, 'but do speak up.'

Clara curtsied low to the Queen – a magnificent, jolly lady whose dress and hair were bejewelled with sweets of every colour.

'Mother, may I present Miss Clara Stahlbaum, whose bravery and quick thinking saved the day!' declared Prince Kracko.

'Welcome, welcome!' cried the Queen, jumping up out of her chair and bustling down the red carpet. 'I hear I have you to thank for

the safe return of my dear Kracko.
Thank you, thank you. A million
times, thank you.' She wrapped
Clara in the warmest of hugs
and laid a large, loud kiss on her
forehead.

With a clap of her hands, the
Sugarplum Fairy summoned hot
chocolate, coffee and tea for the
guests of honour. But the moment
the drinks were set down on the
table, they began to dance! Spanish
chocolate, Arabian coffee and
China tea all danced in their own

distinctive way, the cups spinning on their saucers – but never a drop spilt.

Then the sugar canes came, in candystripe suits of the sort gentlemen wear on the seafront to walk arm in arm with their ladies.

Mrs Bonbon (who always keeps her children under her black-and-white crinoline) let them all loose to dance, and Clara laughed and clapped to see how they did their party-pieces then dived back to the safety of their mother's skirts. The

24

flowers came out to waltz too, on
the greensward – not the sort of
flowers you see in gardens, but the
kind that curl their sugar petals on
the snowy icing of Christmas cakes.
Some snow fell that afternoon,
but it was only a dusting of icing
sugar for, in the Land of Sweets, it
was able to be both Christmas and
summer at the same time.

The prettiest dance of all was the
one the Sugarplum Fairy danced
with her own dashing cavalier.
Clara stared and stared, until Prince

Kracko leaned across and whispered, 'They are in love, you know.' After that, she did not like to stare so very hard, in case she offended them.

'What perfectly beautiful ballet shoes!' exclaimed the Queen, all of a sudden looking at Clara's feet. 'Won't you dance for us too?'

'Oh, *I* can't dance properly! Not yet, at least. These were a Christmas present from my Uncle Drosselmeyer.'

'Oh yes, the dear man. We don't give each other presents at

Christmas here, you know.' Clara
was hardly surprised. The people
of the Lands of Sweets seemed to
have everything they could possibly
want. 'No, instead,' the Queen
went on, 'The fairies grant us each
a Christmas wish. A wish for each
person in the Land of Sweets.'

That gave Prince Kracko an idea.
'Christmas is almost here! And Clara
is in the Land of Sweets. She ought
to be granted a wish!'

Clara blushed as red as the
summer strawberries in her bowl,

27

but the Sugarplum Fairy answered his summons and waved her silvery wand over Clara's head. 'And what is your Christmas wish, my dear?'

Clara did not hesitate for a moment. 'Oh, I wish I could dance just as beautifully as you!' she cried. Prince Kracko rose from his chair and bowed low. He offered her his arm. 'Oh, is it time to go already?' she asked in great disappointment.

The Prince laughed. 'No, but I thought if you were going to dance you might need a partner.'

28

So Prince Kracko and Clara danced – and a more beautiful dance you never saw. For Clara's wish was granted, and she found she was able to dance, in her new shoes, like the best of fairies, like the greatest of ballerinas. While they danced, Kracko looked at her in such a strange way, with his dark, chocolate-coloured eyes, that she felt a little shy and awkward. 'What will *your* Christmas wish be, Prince Kracko?' Clara asked, longing to know.

29

'Oh, simply that I should dance with you again one day, here, in the Land of Sweets, when you are a grown woman.'

They danced and danced. It was the Sugarplum Fairy who had to remind them, 'If Clara doesn't want to miss Christmas at her own house, she had better be going!'

So, sadly, Clara said goodbye to the Queen, and together she and the Prince made the return voyage in their walnut-shell boat. *Swish-*

swirl went the foaming Lemonade Sea, a noise like the moving of pine trees in a winter forest. The snow in the air was so brightly moonlit that she had to close her eyes, and the movement of the boat rocked her, rocked her, rocked her like her new toy Christmas cradle.

When Clara opened her eyes again, her cheek was pressed not to the velvet of the Prince's scarlet jacket but to the plush cushion of the sofa. The damaged nutcracker lay tucked under her arm, while the house still slept in the grey light of a snowy Christmas dawn.

You think she had just been dreaming, don't you?

Then how did Captain Kracko's jaw come to be mended? Good as

new. And why was there a sticky
red kiss right in the middle of
Clara's forehead?

The Mice of Maison Zobrinska

Fiona Dunbar

All right, I know you love *The Nutcracker*. Of course you do: you're a ballet fan! It's just that . . . I hate to break this to you, but the story's not strictly true. So, if you've been pestering your parents to take you on holiday to the Land of Sweets, well, I'm afraid it's going to take them an awfully long time to figure out how to get there.

In case you need reminding, here's the story in a . . . well, in a nutshell: a girl called Clara gets a fancy soldier-shaped nutcracker for Christmas. The nutcracker turns into a handsome prince, and together they triumph over the army of the giant Mouse King, after which the Prince takes Clara off to the Land of Sweets to celebrate, where they are royally

entertained by the Sugarplum Fairy
& co.

Well, if you were that Clara, and
the truth was nothing like that, and
people were always coming up to
you, asking how those mice became
so huge, and whether you married the
Prince or not, you'd get a bit fed up,
wouldn't you? Imagine how it feels for
me, then, answering those questions for
sixty years! Because I *am* Clara, and
I do so wish my Papa's friend, who
wrote the story, hadn't gone round
telling everyone it was about me!

So just for the record, here's what *really* happened . . .

I was eight years old, and we had just moved to the town of Grimschloss. Mama felt I was in need of improving, and with my five little brothers and sisters to care for she was keen to get me out of the house. When she heard of Madame Zobrinska's ballet lessons, she thought this was an excellent solution to both problems.

Madame Zobrinska had once been a prima ballerina and gave

lessons at her grand home on the outskirts of Grimschloss. So it was that one blustery September day I was dispatched to The Outskirts and deposited from our rickety carriage, alone in my scruffy second-hand

tutu, outside the gates of Maison Zobrinska. Grand it may have been, but Maison Zobrinska was very crumbly. It looked as if the ivy covering the walls was the only thing that held the building together. I rang the bell, and was eventually greeted by an equally crumbly butler, who guided me to the salon.

'*Tu es en retard!*' exclaimed Madame Zobrinska, as I hovered in the doorway.

I stared at her blankly, trembling. There were three other girls there,

all much taller and more elegant
than me. 'You're late!' they
chorused gleefully,
translating for
me.

I meekly took
my place alongside
them at the barre.
'Sorry, Madame,' I mumbled.

Bang bang bang! went Madame's
stick on the floor. '*Pliés! Un, deux,
trois . . .*' The large lady at the
piano started playing, and the lesson
began.

Madame was, frankly, terrifying. Her tall white wig contrasted dramatically with her black teeth. Her old-fashioned dress hung limply from her skeletal frame, and her huge hooped skirt swished along the dusty floor as she paraded around, barking out orders in French. Never in a million years could I imagine this old crone as a prima ballerina!

When she wasn't chewing tobacco and spitting it into the fire, Madame Zobrinska would pick up a walnut from a bowl on top of the piano, and crack it open with her fancy soldier-shaped nutcracker. I was sure she only did this to make a sudden, loud noise just when you were least expecting it, so as to throw you off. Your clumsiness would then give her an excuse to hammer on the floor with her stick and go *'Mon Dieu!'* and *'Sacré bleu!'* a lot. It certainly wasn't because she fancied a nut; every time she cracked one it went splintering in all directions. Once I got a shard of nutshell in my eye and Ivy, the pianist, had to clamp

my screaming head under her
sweaty armpit and sloosh my eye
out with spittle.

But even *that*
wasn't the worst
of it.

There were *mice*.

Now, I was known in our
household as the wimp who had
nightmares about mice. Well,
so would you if you'd felt them
nibbling your toes under your
bedclothes on a freezing December
night, as I once did before we

moved to Grimschloss. They
still filled me with terror, and at
Madame Zobrinska's there were
dozens, lurking in the shadows,
their beady little eyes glowing as
they waited for the next nut to be
cracked.

After the first lesson I begged
Mama not to make me go back.

'You must!' cried Mama, as she
bounced my howling twin brothers
on her lap. 'I've already paid for the
term! Besides, you are to perform
for Madame's distinguished guests

at Christmas. It is a great honour!'

Honour? The prospect of dancing for Madame's cronies made me feel ill.

Meanwhile, my mouse nightmares grew worse. They now featured Madame Zobrinska herself as a giant mouse, intent on nibbling me to death with her pointy black teeth. All this worry meant that on my ballet days my insides tied themselves in knots and I was unable to eat a morsel.

45

The other girls, Mimi, Kiki and Fifi, never seemed to be put off by Madame's foul temper, or the flying nut shards, or the mice. They spent their time perfecting their perfect pirouettes, and seemed to understand everything Madame Zobrinska said.

Like when Madame would prod me with her stick, saying, '*Gauche! Gauche!*'

'She thinks you're clumsy,' said Mimi, Kiki and Fifi helpfully.

Another prod from Madame. '*Plus rapide!*'

I looked to the others.

'She wants you to go . . . slower,' they said, giggling.

So I went slower, but Madame only screeched louder, '*Rapidement, rapidement!*'

Mimi, Kiki and Fifi collapsed with laughter. It was then that I realized they had told me the opposite of what Madame meant; she'd wanted me to go *faster*.

This sort of thing happened a lot. And when the girls weren't teasing me, they were bragging about their own ballet skills. This only grew worse as the Christmas party drew near.

'The Grand Duke will be coming!' announced Mimi breathlessly. '*And* he's to present a prize to the best dancer! Well, *I* should win, because I can do the highest "jeté".'

'No, it should be me,' insisted Kiki, 'because *I* can do the finest pirouette.'

'But *my* arabesques are the best,' said Fifi. 'I should win!'

Then the three of them looked at

48

me, and burst into stifled giggles. I rolled my eyes. It wasn't hard to tell what they were thinking.

A week before Christmas, a letter arrived from Madame Zobrinska, reporting that despite early promising signs, I was making little progress. Mama immediately signed me up for another term, even though she couldn't really afford it. 'You must try harder!' she scolded.

I tried harder. We had extra

practice sessions, three times a week;
still I struggled with my 'entrechats'.
As the Christmas party grew nearer,
I was so terrified that I barely ate a
thing. In my dreams, I leaped higher
and higher into the air as I tried
to dodge the gnawing teeth of the
mice and the flying nutshell shards.

The day arrived. I was late, and
got all tangled up in the new tutu
Mama had made for me. Mimi,
Kiki and Fifi giggled. I was so weak
from lack of nourishment, I was
getting spots before my eyes. Little

wonder then that, by the time I had to perform, I stumbled over my entrechat.

There was much dissatisfied murmuring among the noble guests – including, I noticed, the Grand Duke, who sat there resplendent in his military uniform and big white moustache. Madame Zobrinska bared her black teeth at me in disgust from the wings. Trembling, I flitted offstage and out to the grand, crumbly entrance hall, while the others carried on without me.

I needed strength – I needed *food*.

As the crumbly butler was ill in bed, the household was being held together by Ivy – and she was currently playing the piano. This meant I could sneak into the kitchen unobserved, but then I thought with terror of the mice. Spotting Madame Zobrinska's nutcracker hanging on the Christmas tree, I took it as a weapon and followed the mouse droppings downstairs to the kitchen.

There was a sumptuous array of sweetmeats on the kitchen table – along with several small, furry, uninvited guests. I stared at the mice, holding the nutcracker aloft, unable to move a muscle. Cakes, cookies and sweets all beckoned to me; finally I plucked up the courage to advance, gnashing the nutcracker's teeth with a *snap, snap, snap!* all the way.

'*Eek, eek!*' went the mice, as they

scuttled down the table legs and out of the room. At last! I reached out and took a sugared plum from a bowl of candied fruits. As I bit into the delicious sweet, I heard Ivy's voice echoing down the hallway: 'Clara! Where's Clara?' My body sprang back to life as the sugary syrup slipped down my throat. It gave me all the strength I needed; I bounded back up the stairs, dodging the mouse droppings, just in time to take my place for the finale.

I know I was good. I might

have had sticky fingers, but I was
so pumped up, I twirled around
that salon for all I was worth.
And any time Mimi, Kiki or Fifi
tried to upstage me with their
jetés, pirouettes and arabesques, I
mowed them down like a whirling
dervish. Madame Zobrinska's
tobacco-blackened jaw hung open
in disbelief. Finally, I performed my
entrechats, and was able
to stay up long enough
to beat my feet back
and forth six times. Six

55

times! I'd never done that before. I
curtseyed to loud applause.

'Bravo!' exclaimed the Grand
Duke, as he awarded me the prize,
much to the disgust of Mimi, Kiki
and Fifi. I opened the big pink box;
inside was a dear little fluffy white
kitten.

'Oh, how lovely! Thank you!' I
exclaimed.

Everyone gazed at me. I felt I
was expected to take the kitten out
and fondle it, but I couldn't because
of my sticky hands.

Then I had a brilliant idea. 'But,' I added, 'the prize should really go to Madame Zobrinska, for her marvellous teaching.' I held the box out to her, beaming broadly in spite of her suspicious scowl.

Why did I give away such a darling prize? Well, as I had hoped, the cat turned out to be a splendid mouser. I may have had to continue with my lessons at Madame Zobrinska's, but the mice were soon a thing of the past. Hurrah!

What's that? You want to know

57

why there's no Prince? My, you're
hard to please, aren't you! Well,
you may like to know that my
triumph at Madame Zobrinska's was
the beginning of a glittering career,
and I performed in *The Nutcracker*
for many years – opposite a 'prince'
whom I eventually married! We
are too old and grey now for those
magical journeys to the Land of
Sweets, but he still gives me
sugarplums at Christmas
time.

Bunty's Dream

Ian Billings

MRS SLEE'S WONDERFUL CIRCUS
OF MARVELS!

read the poster on the village notice
board and underneath that it said:

THREE WEEKS TO GO

The children of the village
were very excited, for this was the
greatest circus in the world. They
were even more excited a week later
to see the words changed to:

TWO WEEKS TO GO

The village was full of expectation.
The children were thinking
of trapeze artistes instead of
concentrating on their school work,
the baker was burning his bread
while dreaming of acrobats and
the milkman was so lost in thought

60

about the jugglers that he smashed three bottles by accident.

So, you can imagine how the villagers felt when the poster was changed to:

ONE WEEK TO GO

Nobody could sleep. Every conversation was about the circus.

'Biggest one in the world, I heard!' said someone.

'Thirteen clowns and seventy custard pies!' said someone else.

'Highest circus tent in Europe,

61

apparently!' said another.

Finally the day came
when the village woke,
rubbed its eyes and
found – a circus tent. It sat
proudly on the village green with its
big yellow and red sides and bright
red and yellow flags flapping merrily
in the breeze.

Before many of the villagers had
even changed out of their pyjamas
a queue started to appear at the
ticket office. It was a queue that got
longer and longer and longer.

★

Bunty was curled up and fast asleep, dreaming the happiest of happy dreams. She was snoring softly and imagining a place far, far away. A place where she could run and dance and skip freely, where she could laugh and sing without care. Suddenly she woke with a jolt. Someone was banging on the bars of her cage.

'Get in the ring in three minutes!' snarled a voice.

She shook her head and

remembered – she was still locked in a cage, she was still working for the circus and, looking at her reflection in a dirty puddle, she was still a walrus.

Meanwhile, the crowds flooded in. They scurried across the scattered sawdust and found the best places they could on the dirty wooden benches. The Gwen Miller Orchestra played jangly music and the clowns lolloped around the aisles with oversized water pistols and buckets of confetti.

64

Soon the real performance began. Jugglers juggled, acrobats spun and twisted and custard pies flew through the air. The audience adored it, but behind the curtain there was a different scene.

Mrs Slee, a small woman with black hair in a tight bun, was angrily tapping her cane on the ground. Mrs Slee was not happy.

'Hopeless!' she sneered as each performer came backstage. 'Every one of you is hopeless!'

The clowns looked sheepishly at

each other, the human cannonball looked like he might explode and the owner of the flea circus just scratched himself.

Mrs Slee strode back and forth behind the curtains. The sawdust crackled under her feet.

'This is the greatest circus in the world. This should therefore be the greatest performance in the world!'

She leaned over to Bobo the clown, squeezed his red nose and grimaced. 'But it is not!'

Yes, Mrs Slee was a fearsome

woman. No one dared cross her, for they knew that if they did, they would find themselves without a job or, worse, clearing out the elephants' enclosure.

'Thank goodness I have my walrus!'

She whipped her cane in the air, the musicians played a fanfare and her star performer waddled into the centre of the ring.

'Bunty!' hissed Mrs Slee, laughing her dark, black laugh. 'Do your stuff!'

Bunty the walrus had worked for Mrs Slee for many years and her act was very well rehearsed. She knew exactly what she was doing, and she usually charmed the audience without fail. Until tonight. Tonight, Bunty was lost in thought, dreaming of a happier place and dreaming of her freedom. Before the astonished eyes of the audience everything that could go wrong with her act did go wrong. She forgot to clap, she missed the fish that was thrown to her, she forgot to honk her horn to the music. The audience clapped politely, but secretly they wanted the clowns back.

'That was a disaster!' shrieked Mrs Slee as Bunty crawled back into her cage after the show. 'What happened?'

Bunty shrugged.

'Don't you shrug at me!' squealed Mrs Slee, smacking the side of the cage with her cane. Bunty curled herself into a ball and looked sad.

Mrs Slee slammed the door shut

and pressed her face against the bars. It was a face full of anger, frustration and spots. Her nose quivered in fury.

'Get it right tomorrow or it won't be the bars I'll be beating!'

And she stomped off back to her office, where Bunty could hear a bottle being opened and a cigar being lit.

The walrus lay quietly in her cage listening to the circus slowly putting itself to bed. She waited until every cage and caravan door had been closed and locked. She waited until she could hear the elephants snoring and muttering in their dreams and Gwen Miller humming herself to sleep.

Only then did Bunty slip a small tatty piece of newspaper from under her dirty old pillow and carefully unfold it. She held it up to the moonlight that was streaming into her cage and gazed at the picture. It was a small black and white photograph of a ballet dancer. (The caption read, 'World-famous

7

ballerina Margarita Flipova,' but
of course Bunty could not read it.)
Bunty gazed at the photo for a few
minutes before slowly folding it up
again and pushing it back under
her pillow. She was going to have a
wonderful dream tonight.

The ringing phone woke Bunty very
early the next morning. Her bright
eyes flicked open and she could
make out the silhouette of Mrs Slee
in her office, picking up the phone.

'Slee's Circus. Mrs Slee speaking

. . . Hello there, London Zoo, thank you for getting back to me . . . Yes, I certainly do have a walrus for sale . . . Her circus days are over . . . How much do I want? What do you usually pay? . . . Goodness that's a handsome price . . . It's a deal! . . . And I'll deliver her myself.'

Mrs Slee put down the phone, found a big dirty sack and walked towards the animal enclosures. She shone a torch into the dark corners of Bunty's cage. Imagine

73

her surprise when she realized it was completely empty!

As soon as Bunty had heard the word 'zoo' she had decided to get away. She'd heard many horrible stories about zoos. Once a performing giraffe told her, 'We're lucky to be in a circus, Bunty. My mother was in a zoo for sixteen years and she got stared at by humans all day long. At least we only have to put up with three audiences a day. And we get to play with the clowns. We're lucky we are, Bunty!'

Mrs Slee's Circus was bad but the zoo sounded much, much worse.

So Bunty wrapped two kippers in her treasured newspaper cutting and squeezed out of her cage. (This was surprisingly easy and she wondered why she hadn't tried it before.) She waddled out of the circus and down the road to who knows where. By the time Mrs Slee had organized the clowns into a search party Bunty was far, far away and feeling much, much happier.

★

Bunty walked and waddled for miles and miles through rain and storms, cold and snow. Finally she found herself in a big, big city feeling exhausted and very, very hungry. She sat on the pavement as huge cars zoomed passed. Both her kippers were long gone but she tried not to feel too dejected. Suddenly a car stopped and the window was wound down. A man poked his face out.

'You lost?'

Bunty nodded her head.

'You hungry?'

Bunty nodded again.

'Catch!'

The man threw an apple and Bunty caught it in her mouth.

'Wow!' said the man before driving off. 'You should be in the circus!'

That evening Bunty found herself sheltering under a huge grey bridge. She could hear the traffic zooming back and forth above her head. She could see the twinkling lights of the city reflected in the river and, as

she looked at her own reflection in
another dirty puddle, she wondered
if she had made the right decision.

Later that night Bunty waddled
into a dark alleyway and
rummaged for some fishy nibbles
in a rubbish bin, before huddling
in a doorway that was sheltered
from the wind. She snuggled
down into a wet puddle and,
using her mouth, dragged a sheet
of cardboard over herself. As she
placed her head against the door,
she sighed, studied her newspaper

clipping for comfort and drifted
off to sleep. She was in the middle
of a lovely dream full of ribbons
and dresses and ballet music and
dancing when she was woken by
a creaking followed by a cracking
followed by the sound of breaking
wood! With a crash, the door Bunty
was leaning against broke open
and she fell into the building behind
her! She started barking in surprise
but was interrupted by a wonderful
sound, coming from deep inside the
building. It was music, beautiful,

gorgeous, *happy* music. Bunty started swaying her head back and forth to the rhythms and her flipper beat the ground. It was the loveliest sound she had ever heard – far better than the tatty tunes from the circus. This was the music of her dreams. Bunty looked out into the cold, wet alleyway then at the dark, mysterious corridor – and it did not take her long to decide which way to go.

She waddled up the corridor and as she waddled the music grew

80

louder and louder and more and
more powerful. At the end of the
corridor light was blazing out from
the edges of a door. Bunty turned
the handle with her mouth and
there, on the other side, was the
backstage of a theatre!

Bunty could not believe her eyes.
The place was a blaze of colour
and light – a completely different
world to the dingy, straw-scattered
old circus. The frilliest of tutus were
displayed on a rail, ropes hung
in hanks waiting to be used and

beautifully painted scenery was leaning against the walls. But that was not all. When Bunty placed her eager snout between a gap in the velvety curtains she could see right out on to the stage. And what she saw was the happiest sight of her life. A ballet was being performed. Hundreds of dancers were swirling and turning gracefully to the beautiful melodies. Bunty stared, transfixed, and the two hours of the performance flew by without Bunty moving from her spot. Finally, the show ended, the audience applauded and the stage was covered in flowers. As the lead ballerina curtsied, Bunty gasped in recognition. Those fine long legs and that black, black hair – it was none other than Margarita Flipova!

As the conductor took his bow, he turned to the first violinist and said, 'Did I just hear a walrus bark?' The violinist looked at him as if he was mad.

★

83

That night Bunty found a quiet corner of the theatre. She curled up on a pile of old rope and had the best sleep she'd ever had.

For three blissful weeks Bunty hid herself away in the theatre and night after night watched the ballet being performed. The dancer she watched most was Margarita Flipova, and she would twirl and twist and turn in the wings, copying every graceful, elegant move. Bunty knew she was just a clumsy old circus walrus – but as she practised and practised and practised she began to wonder if she could be something more.

One night, the audience had shuffled into the theatre as usual and the smell of expensive perfume filled the air. Tickets had sold out quickly and everyone was particularly excited because this was to be Margarita Flipova's final performance. And no one was more excited than Bunty. She took up her position in the wings and

stared out at the stage. She watched
the stage crew making the final
preparations. She heard the orchestra
tuning up. But then she saw something
that did not usually happen. Margarita
Flipova's dresser was looking very
concerned as she spoke to the stage
manager. The stage manager started
looking very concerned and turned
to talk to the theatre director. The
theatre director slapped his forehead in
disbelief and was soon in conversation
with the conductor who broke his
baton in surprise!

What was the matter? Bunty continued to stare blankly. Everyone backstage was starting to look bothered and unsure of what to do. Finally, the theatre director made a decision. He pushed his way through the curtain and addressed the audience.

'Ladies and gentlemen, welcome to the Ballet Theatre. I have some terrible, terrible news!'

He produced a handkerchief and blew his nose loudly.

'The star of our show, Margarita Flipova, has had an accident!'

The audience gasped in disbelief.

'Whilst climbing out of the bath she slipped on some stupidly placed ice-cream, skidded on some lettuce left by an admirer and as we speak seven firemen are attempting to pull her head out of a drawer!'

An even bigger gasp ran round the audience.

'And so there will be no final performance tonight!'

The audience fell silent, but then

some chatting started up and the chatting became whinging and whinging became moaning. A small man with a very fine suit and greased hair stood up and said, 'Can't anyone else dance the ballet?'

The audience clapped and muttered in agreement.

The theatre director looked flustered – he was not used to talking to audiences, especially ones that talked back.

'We have no understudies. No one can take over.'

He blew his nose again while he thought.

'Unless, of course, there is anyone here who can dance the ballet!'

There was a silence. Everyone in the audience looked at everyone else in the audience, but no one was going to volunteer.

And then the theatre was filled with the loudest, happiest bark ever heard. Everyone wondered where it had come from, but they didn't wonder for long as on to the stage waddled Bunty the Walrus – and she was wearing

a tutu!

The

audience

gasped again

and stared in

disbelief. The

theatre director fiddled with his

handkerchief and the conductor

leaned towards the first violinist and

said, 'I *told* you I heard a walrus!'

Bunty assumed her pose in the

centre of the stage. The theatre

director nodded at the conductor

and the orchestra struck up with
the opening chords of the music.
This was the moment Bunty had
waited for all her life. Her cue
came and the audience sat amazed
and delighted as she began to
dance. It was step for step, waddle
for waddle, the same as Margarita
Flipova. Each movement was
perfect. She swooped gracefully
across the stage with her flippers
flapping like a professional. She
pivoted on her tail as if she had
done it all her life. Her snout was

held high as she leaped and twirled
through scene after scene and by
the time the ballet ended a new star
had been born.

The flowers the audience had
brought for Margarita Flipova now
fell at the walrus's flippers. The
audience roared with delight and
Bunty performed again and again.
As the curtain came down for
the final time the theatre director
was standing by to offer Bunty a
contract to star in their next ballet
and remain with the company as

long as she liked. Bunty couldn't say no. All she asked for was her own room, a soft pillow and a bucket of kippers.

And from that day on Bunty became the most famous ballet-dancing walrus in the world. She toured all over America, Europe and the Far East and she performed to kings and queens and presidents. Instead of staring at her reflection in a muddy puddle she now stared at her reflection in a sparkling dressing-room mirror. And soon

little girls everywhere were carrying
around newspaper cuttings of their
idol, Bunty the ballerina!

The Magic Shoes

Julia Donaldson

'Hey, you! Yes, you! Turn round, look over your shoulder,' sang Ellen's brother, Luke, into the microphone.

Ellen was sitting in the village hall watching Luke's band, Breakneck, rehearse for the Battle of the Bands.

The hall was nearly empty, but that evening it would be packed with fans of the six different bands who were entering the competition.

As well as being Breakneck's singer, Luke wrote most of their songs, including this one.

'It's me! Yes, me! Turn round, I'm still here,' he sang. Then he wandered moodily around the stage, while the lead guitarist, Steph, played a twangy solo.

Steph, who never smiled, wore frayed black trousers with a pointless

97

chain hanging out of the pocket and a black T-shirt with orange flames on it. The solo went on and on.

'Steph's so good at the guitar,' Ellen whispered to Steph's sister Seraphina, who was sitting next to her.

'I know,' said Seraphina. She was two years older than Ellen and dressed very much like her brother, except that her T-shirt had a silver skull on it. 'But I bet they don't win. I don't think they should have chosen this song. It's not going to get people dancing. Steph wrote a much better one called "Savage".'

Ellen couldn't imagine Steph writing anything dancy, but she was quite shy of Seraphina and didn't say so. Besides, she had just remembered something.

'Dancing – help! I'm going to be late for ballet!' She picked up a bag from the floor.

'You've got the wrong bag – that's mine,' said Seraphina, who also went to ballet, but to a later class.

'Sorry.' Ellen grabbed her own bag and hurried to the door.

At least she didn't have far to go. The ballet classes were held in a room called the studio, which was above the hall. Ellen ran up the stairs. The changing room was empty. The other girls must be in the studio already, but Ellen couldn't hear any music so the class couldn't have started yet.

Hurriedly, she put on her leotard and ballet shoes and scooped her hair into the hairnet that Madame

Jolie, the ballet teacher,
insisted they all wear.
Madame Jolie was
very fussy about how
they looked and could
pounce on a girl for the smallest
thing, such as crossing the ribbons
on her ballet shoes in the wrong
way.

Ellen was just giving herself
a quick check in the full-length
mirror when a voice said, 'What's
happened to your feet?'

It was a voice that she knew very

well. It was coming from the mirror
and belonged to Princess Mirror-
Belle.

Ellen and Mirror-Belle had met
several times before. Mirror-Belle
looked just like Ellen's reflection,
but instead of staying in the mirror
as reflections usually do, she had a
habit of coming out of it. She was
much cheekier and naughtier than
Ellen, and she was always boasting
about her life in the palace and the
magic things that she said happened
to her.

Ellen hadn't seen Mirror-Belle for a while, and she wasn't sure how pleased she was to see her now. All too often Mirror-Belle had got them both into trouble and then escaped into a mirror leaving Ellen to take the blame.

'Mirror-Belle! You can't come to my dancing class,' she said now. Then added, 'What do you mean about my feet anyway? What's wrong with them?'

'They're not dancing!' said Princess Mirror-Belle, leaping out

of the mirror into the changing

room. She was wearing an identical

leotard and ballet shoes to Ellen's

and a hairnet too, though she pulled

this off and flung it to the ground

with a shudder, saying, 'I must have

104

walked through a spider's web.'
Then she began to prance around
the room, pointing her toes and
waving her arms.

'Stop! You'll tire yourself out
before the class has even started,'
said Ellen.

'I can't stop. I'm surprised that
you can. I think you should take
your shoes back to the elves and
complain.'

'What elves?' asked Ellen.

But already Mirror-Belle had
opened the door to the studio and

105

was dancing in. Ellen followed her with a sinking feeling.

The other girls in the class were standing in a line, waiting to curtsy to Madame Jolie. Ellen and Mirror-Belle joined the line. Some of the girls tittered as Mirror-Belle continued to dance up and down on the spot.

'Who's she?' asked one.

'She looks just like you, Ellen,' said another.

Madame Jolie had been talking to the lady who played the piano, but now she turned round to face the class.

'*Bonjour, mes élèves*,' she said.

This meant 'Good day, my pupils' in French. Madame Jolie was French and she always started the class like this.

'*Bonjour, Madame*,' chanted Ellen and the other girls as they dropped a curtsy to the teacher – all except Mirror-Belle, who twirled around with her arms above her head.

'Leetle girl on ze left – zat ees not a curtsy,' said Madame Jolie.

107

'Ah, you noticed – well done.' Mirror-Belle jiggled about as she spoke. 'No, I *never* curtsy – except very occasionally to my parents, the King and Queen. And I'm surprised that all these girls are curtsying to you instead of me – or are you a princess too?'

'Zees ees not ze comedy class,' replied Madame. Then her frown deepened. 'Where ees your 'airnet?' she asked.

'A *hairnet,* did you say? Why on earth should I wear one of those?

108

The only thing I ever put on my head is a crown. I didn't wear one today, though, because . . .' Mirror-Belle paused for a second and then went on, 'because one of the diamonds fell out of it yesterday and it had to go to the palace jeweller to be repaired.'

Ellen wondered if this was true. She had never seen Mirror-Belle with a crown and sometimes doubted if she really *was* a princess.

'If you forget ze 'airnet one more time you will leave ze class,' warned

Madame. Then she ordered the girls to go to the barre.

'We will practise ze "pliés". First position, everyone.'

Ellen and the others held the barre with their right hands and, with their heels together, turned their toes out. Then, as the piano started up, they all bent their knees and straightened up again. Ellen couldn't see Mirror-Belle, who was behind her, but she could bear a thumping sound and some stifled giggles.

'*Non, non, non!*' exclaimed Madame. She clapped her hands to stop the music and then wagged her finger at Mirror-Belle. 'Why ees it zat you are jumping? I said plié, not "sauté". A plié is a bend. A sauté is a jump.' She demonstrated the two movements gracefully.

'It's no use telling me that,' said Mirror-Belle, leaving the barre and dancing up to Madame. 'It's my ballet shoes you should be talking to.'

Some of the girls giggled, and

Madame was not impressed. 'Do not argue, and keep still!' she ordered Mirror-Belle.

'But I can't!' Mirror-Belle complained. 'I did think that *you* might understand about my shoes, even if Ellen doesn't. I can see I'll have to explain.'

'Zere is no need for zat,' said Madame, but Mirror-Belle ignored her.

Skipping around in time to her own words, she said, 'They're magic shoes. As soon as I put them on, my feet start dancing and I can't stop till the soles are worn out.' She twirled round and then added, 'Sometimes I dance all night.'

'Then why aren't they worn out already?' asked one of the girls, and received a glare from Madame.

'This is a new pair,' said Mirror-Belle. 'Some elves crept into the palace and made them for me in the night. I hid behind a curtain and watched them. Luckily they didn't see me. If they found out I knew about them, they'd probably never come back. They're very shy, you see.' She leaped in the air and landed with a thump. 'This pair is very well made. They'll probably take ages to wear out.'

Madame had had enough. 'In zat case, you can go and wear zem out somewhere else,' she said angrily.

'What a good idea,' said Mirror-Belle. 'So you're not just a pretty pair of feet after all,' and she flitted and twirled her way to the door.

114

'Come on, Ellen!' she called over her shoulder as she danced out of the room.

Ellen hesitated. Part of her wanted to follow Mirror-Belle, to try to stop her causing too much chaos elsewhere. On the other hand, she never was very good at that; usually she just got drawn into whatever trouble Mirror-Belle created. She decided to stay where she was. With a bit of luck, Mirror-Belle might get bored and go back through the changing-room mirror into her own world.

115

'What an *enfant terrible*!' muttered Madame. 'And no 'airnet!' she added, as if this was the worst crime of all. Then she turned back to the class. 'Now, *mes élèves*, we will do ze pliés in second position.'

Ellen's mother, Mrs Page, was teaching the piano to Robert Rumbold when the doorbell rang.

'Excuse me, Robert,' she said, interrupting a piece called 'Boogie Woogie Bedbug', which Robert was playing very woodenly. She went to the door.

'Ellen, you're back very early – and why are you still in your dancing things?'

'I'm not Ellen, I'm Princess Mirror-Belle,' said the girl on the doorstep. She danced past Ellen's mother and into the sitting room.

'Don't be silly, Ellen. And come out of there. You know you're not allowed in the sitting room when I'm teaching.'

Ellen's mother had never met

117

Mirror-Belle before. Although Ellen was always talking about her, her mother thought she was just an imaginary friend.

Robert was still playing 'Boogie Woogie Bedbug', and the girl who Mrs Page thought was Ellen was slinking around the room, waggling her hips and clicking her fingers in time to the music.

'You heard me, Ellen. Go to your room and get changed. Where are your clothes anyway?'

'That's a tricky question. It

depends on whether my maid is having a lazy day or not. If she is, then my clothes are still on the palace floor where I left them. If she's not, then they're hanging up in the royal wardrobe,' said the girl, jumping on to the sofa and off again.

'I suppose you've left them at ballet,' said Mrs Page with a sigh. 'You'd better go back there now and get changed.'

'That's really no way to talk to a princess, but since you're my friend's mother I'll excuse you.' She danced out of the room and Ellen's mother heard the front door slam.

'I'm so sorry about that, Robert,' she said.

Robert just grunted and went on playing 'Boogie Woogie Bedbug'. Strangely enough, the piece was now sounding much livelier than before, as if the bedbug had learned to jump at last.

'That's coming on so much better,' Mrs Page told him as she saw him out a few minutes later.

'Keep practising it, and then next week you can start on "Hip Hop Hippo".'

Just then she spotted Ellen coming round the corner towards the house. She was wearing her outdoor clothes.

'Hello, Ellen — that was very quick! You're back just in time to apologize to Robert.'

'What for?' asked Ellen, looking puzzled.

'For barging into his lesson like that.'

'Oh no, don't say Mirror-Belle's

121

been here,' groaned Ellen. 'Where is she now?'

'She's in your imagination – just the same as usual – so stop blaming her for everything you do wrong. In fact, if you mention Mirror-Belle one more time I won't let you go to the Battle of the Bands.'

That evening Ellen, who had succeeded in not mentioning Mirror-Belle (though she kept thinking about her), was standing near the front of the village hall waiting for the second half of the Battle of the Bands to start. Three of the bands had played already, and the last of these, Hellhole, had received wild applause. Breakneck would have to play really well to beat them.

'Do you want a Coke?' came a voice. It was Seraphina, who had pushed her way through the crowds of people to join Ellen.

'Thanks. I like

your T-shirt – it's cool,' said Ellen.

Seraphina was no longer wearing her skull T-shirt. This one had a green-winged snake on it.

'Did you hear what happened to my other one?' asked Seraphina. 'It was stolen from the changing room while I was at ballet class. So were my jeans. Who do you think could have taken them?'

'I've no idea,' said Ellen untruthfully.

In fact, she had a very strong suspicion.

Mirror-Belle must have danced back to the hall while the older girls were having their lesson and changed into Seraphina's black jeans and silver-skull T-shirt. But where was she now?'

Just then the lights in the hall were dimmed and some bright-coloured ones came on over the stage.

'Hi there, pop-pickers! Welcome back to the battlefield!' said the compère, Mr Wilks, who was a geography teacher in Luke's school.

Seraphina sniggered. 'He's not exactly cool, is he?' she whispered.

Ellen decided she didn't like the superior way in which Seraphina always spoke. Mirror-Belle put on airs too, but at least she could be good fun. Ellen wondered again where she had got to.

'Put your paws together for Breakneck!' said Mr Wilks, and Ellen clapped much louder than anyone else as Luke, Steph and the other members of Breakneck slouched on to the stage.

Luke tripped up on his way to his place and everyone laughed. Ignoring them, he hunched over the microphone.

'Hey, you! Yes, you!' he began.

He was pointing at the audience, and Ellen thought he looked quite good, but she could hear him only very faintly. Then he stopped altogether and signalled to Steph and the others to stop playing. What had gone wrong?

The sound technician came on to the stage, sighed and plugged the

127

lead from Luke's microphone into the amplifier.

'It must have come unplugged when he tripped,' said Seraphina.

Not looking too put out, Luke started again.

'Hey you! Yes, you! Turn round, look over your shoulder,' he sang.

A loud screeching sound accompanied his voice.

'Feedback,' whispered Seraphina knowledgeably.

This time, Luke didn't stop. The sound technician fiddled about with a knob and soon Luke's voice sounded normal. In fact, he was singing really well, Ellen thought, though she probably wouldn't admit it to him afterwards. But it had not been a good beginning. Some of the audience were still laughing, and a couple of Hellhole fans tried to start up a chant of, 'Get them off!'

Breakneck didn't let any of this upset them. They carried on, and by the time Steph's twangy guitar solo started quite a few people were tapping their feet and swaying. The

129

coloured lights were flashing and some smoke started to rise from the foot of the stage.

'That's a smoke machine,' said Seraphina. 'It was Steph's idea.'

The guitar solo came to an end at last and Luke started the 'Hey, you!' chorus again.

Ellen was aware of a disturbance somewhere behind her.

'Watch out!'

'Stop pushing!'

'That was my toe!'

She turned round and saw who

130

was creating the fuss and bother. It was a girl dressed in black, dancing her way through the crowds. Because she was flinging her arms around, people were making way for her and soon she was at the very front of the hall.

'Turn round,' sang Luke, and the girl turned round, her loose hair flying about.

'Look over your shoulder,' he sang, and she stuck her chin out over her right shoulder, at the same time stamping her right foot and raising her left hand. Her wild hair was almost covering her face, but Ellen had no doubt who it was.

'Mirror-Belle, how could you?' she muttered under her breath. Just when Breakneck were beginning to impress people . . . This would ruin their chances!

But, to her surprise, a couple of girls in the front row started copying Mirror-Belle's movements, turning round whenever she did, looking over their shoulders with the same stamp and hand gesture, and pointing whenever Luke sang 'Hey, you!' Some people stared at them, but others began to join in.

The dance was infectious. Very soon nearly everyone in front of Ellen seemed to be doing it. They were joining in the words of the song as well. She turned round and saw that people behind her were dancing and singing too.

On the stage, Luke was grinning. He caught Steph's eye and mouthed something to her. Ellen knew that they were at the end of the song, but they weren't slowing down like they usually did.

'They've gone back to the beginning! They're going to sing it all over again!' she whispered to Seraphina happily.

She expected Seraphina to look happy too but instead she was staring accusingly at Mirror-Belle.

'Have you seen what I have?' she asked. 'She's wearing my clothes! She's the thief!'

She strode forward, pushing through the dancers in front of her and reaching out for the skull T-shirt, which looked more like a dress on Mirror-Belle. Just when Seraphina tried to grab it, Mirror-Belle did another of her spins and, for the first time, noticed Ellen behind her.

'Oh, hello, Ellen. Why didn't you come with me? I've been visiting your local library. It hasn't got nearly so many books as the palace library, but that's quite good in a way, because it meant there was lots of room for dancing about. I must

135

say, though, some of the servants in there are awfully rude.'

So that's where Mirror-Belle had been! Now Ellen would dread going to the library, knowing that the librarians would think she was the naughty dancing girl they had told off.

Meanwhile, the rest of the audience were so carried away with the song and dance that they didn't spot that Mirror-Belle had stopped doing the actions along with them. They took no notice of her – apart from Seraphina, that is, who was making another grab at the T-shirt.

Mirror-Belle was too quick for her. 'Excuse me,' she said, 'my shoes are taking off again!' and the next moment she was dancing her way back through the crowds.

Seraphina followed her, and Ellen followed Seraphina. The rest of the audience just went on dancing in time to the music — almost as if they were all wearing magic shoes themselves.

'Where's she gone?' asked
Seraphina.

They were out of the hall now
and Mirror-Belle was nowhere to be
seen.

'Let's look outside,' suggested
Ellen.

In fact, she was pretty sure that
Mirror-Belle would be on her way
to the nearest mirror, the one in
the changing room upstairs, but she
wanted to give her a little time to
escape from Seraphina. She felt a bit
guilty about this – after all, Mirror-

Belle had taken Seraphina's clothes – but she couldn't help being on Mirror-Belle's side.

They peered out of the front door and up and down the street.

'No,' said Seraphina. 'Anyway, she wouldn't go outside – she was wearing ballet shoes.'

You don't know Mirror-Belle, thought Ellen, but said nothing.

'Let's look upstairs,' said Seraphina, and she led the way.

'Look! There are my clothes on the floor!' she cried as they entered the changing room. She picked them up. 'They're drenched in sweat!' she said in disgust. 'You'd think she'd been dancing ever since she put them on. Here, you hold them, Ellen – I'm going to find her.'

Seraphina strode into the studio, but emerged a few moments later, looking puzzled. 'That's funny,' she said. 'She's not in there, and there's no other way out.' Then, 'Why are you smiling?' she asked Ellen, who was glancing at the mirror.

Ellen didn't want to tell Seraphina

that she knew Mirror-Belle had gone. She would have to explain her smile some other way.

'I'm smiling,' she said, 'because I'm sure Breakneck are going to win the Battle of the Bands.'

Then she turned back to the mirror and quietly, so that Seraphina wouldn't hear, she whispered, 'Thanks, Mirror-Belle.'

141

Giselle

Belinda Hollyer

Once, in a small
village in Germany,
on the edge of
a grand Silesian
estate, there lived a
beautiful girl by the
name of Giselle. Not

only beautiful, but kind as well, the young girl enjoyed the love and protection of the villagers. Giselle's mother cherished her only child, and took great care of her for her health was delicate.

Giselle's fragile beauty and loving nature gained her many admirers, and two young men in particular hoped to win both her heart and her hand in marriage. One was Hilarion, a local forester who had known Giselle all her life. The other was a mysterious young man called Loys, a newcomer to the village. The forester was jealous of the dashing Loys and the ease with which he seemed to have charmed his way into Giselle's affections. Hilarion suspected Loys of being more than he seemed, and kept a careful watch on him whenever he could.

The truth was more extraordinary than Hilarion could have imagined. Loys was not a peasant at all,

144

but Albrecht, Duke of Silesia. The young nobleman had seen Giselle in the forest one day and had fallen helplessly in love with her. He had come to the village to court her, disguised as a peasant, because he was afraid the beautiful young girl wouldn't take his love seriously if she knew his true identity.

Early one morning, Albrecht returned to the village from a secret trip to his castle home. All was quiet and the village deserted, for almost everyone was hard at work harvesting grapes. Albrecht and his squire Wilfrid thought they were alone: neither noticed Hilarion hiding, watching them intently, his brow furrowed in thought: what was a peasant doing with a sword – and who was his finely dressed companion?

Wilfrid had always been uneasy about Albrecht's deception, and once more he pleaded with his master to return to the palace and forget about Giselle. But to no avail: Albrecht could not bring himself to abandon his love, nor yet to reveal his true identity to her. For the time being, he would have to remain disguised as Loys.

Leaving his cloak and sword in his cottage, the young Duke dismissed his servant and went with a smile to knock on Giselle's door. Then, quickly, Albrecht hid from view. He knew that Giselle would be at home – for she was too delicate to work in the fields, and had learned instead to weave and spin – and he wanted to tease her a little.

Out peeped Giselle, remembering
that Loys would return that day
and eager to welcome her charming
suitor. He must be hiding, she
decided and, pretending not to care,
she began to dance and hum to
herself, all the while secretly trying
to find out where Loys was.

She paused in her dance for a
moment. She was sure she could
hear a sound . . . Yes! From his
hiding place, Loys was blowing her
kisses! Giselle still couldn't see him,
so she decided to sulk. That should

do the trick. And, sure enough, as Giselle turned with a flounce to her cottage door, there was Loys beside her, smiling broadly and holding out his hands. Albrecht felt a rush of love at being close to his dear Giselle once more. Perhaps, after all, now *was* the right moment to declare his love for her.

He led the young girl to a bench beside the cottage. Taking her hand in his, Albrecht confessed his eternal love. 'I swear that I love you, that I will always love you,' he said softly.

149

'Can I hope that you might love me too?'

Giselle wanted to be completely sure of Loys's affections. Picking a daisy from the grass, she began airily to pluck the petals off, one at a time. 'He loves me, he loves me not,' she murmured, hardly daring to glance at Loys's face. 'He loves me, he loves me not.' As the last petal fell to the ground, Giselle burst into nervous tears. 'He loves me not!' But Albrecht, picking up the flower, showed her that she had

missed the last petal of all: one
'he loves me' petal remained.
Giselle beamed through her tears
and began to dance once
more, accompanied by the
jubilant Albrecht.

From his hiding place,
Hilarion had seen
everything and his heart
burned in anger to see
Giselle so happy with Loys.
He leaped in front of them and
wrenched them apart with a cry of
rage. The startled Giselle frowned

indignantly at Hilarion. 'How dare you!' she exclaimed.

Crushed by her reproach, Hilarion fell clumsily to his knees. 'My sweet Giselle,' he begged, gazing up at her lovely face, 'I'm the only one who truly loves you! Trust only me!'

But Giselle's patience was at an end. How dare Hilarion embarrass her in this way? And he looked so foolish kneeling there, so unlike her dashing Loys. 'I think you had better go, Hilarion. I have nothing more to say to you.'

Hilarion stared up at her in dismay and pulled himself miserably to his feet. Filled with shame, the wretched forester rushed away. Loys held Giselle tenderly in his arms. He did love her: she was sure of that now. And she loved him too.

By the time her friends returned from the vineyards, laden with baskets of grapes, Giselle's spirits had lifted. She joined her friends in their dancing and singing, and the sweethearts were a picture of happiness.

Her attention attracted by all

the commotion, Giselle's mother
glanced out of her window. Giselle!
Dancing! She rushed to remonstrate
her daughter. Didn't Giselle
remember that she was much too
delicate to leap about? She should
be resting more, and dancing less.
Reluctantly, Giselle returned to her
cottage with her mother, and one
by one the villagers returned to their
afternoon's work.

Hilarion returned to the village
a few minutes later, still burning
with anger at his rejection. He

was determined to prove that his
suspicions about Loys were correct.
Suddenly he heard a hunting horn:
a hunting party was approaching.
He knew he must act quickly and
slipped into Loys's cottage. Perhaps,
he thought, I'll find some proof there
that Loys has been lying.

The noble party entered the
village, led by Wilfrid, Albrecht's
squire. Unable to persuade the
hunting party to choose another
place to rest, he feared that
Albrecht's identity would be

discovered. But no: Albrecht was nowhere to be seen and Wilfrid breathed a sigh of relief.

The Prince of Courland and his daughter Bathilde, along with huntsmen and other members of the court, dismounted. Refreshments were needed, and now! Knowing no one else in the village would be home, Wilfrid knocked with some trepidation at Giselle's door. As soon as her mother saw who had arrived she bustled around, preparing food and drink and setting up a table and chairs in the shade of a tree for the royal visitors.

Giselle's curiosity soon got the better of her shyness and it wasn't long before she joined in. A hunting party from the palace was too exciting to miss! Bathilde in particular was touched by Giselle's unaffected nature – and when she discovered that she and the peasant girl were both to marry soon, decided to give Giselle a present. After a quick word with her father Bathilde took a pretty necklace

from round her own neck, and
hung it round Giselle's. Giselle had
never owned anything so beautiful,
and she kissed Bathilde's hand in
delighted gratitude. What a treasure
to show Loys!

Bathilde decided to rest in Giselle's
cottage for a time while the hunt
continued. A hunting horn was
left outside so that she could call
when she was ready to join them.
The hunting party departed and all
was quiet again. Hilarion peered
triumphantly from Loys's cottage.

He had found the sword, and at last could show that Loys was not who he said he was. But, hearing Giselle's friends returning from the vineyards, Hilarion hid. He wanted to choose his moment carefully.

The villagers persuaded Giselle's mother to allow her daughter to dance with them – 'But only for a short while, mind you.' Albrecht joined them, and the dance ended with the two lovers embracing, delighted to show their newfound love to all.

159

This was too much for Hilarion. He rushed from his hiding place, all thought of timing forgotten. Blind with rage, he thrust the sword into Giselle's startled grasp.

'There!' he shouted. 'You see, Loys is not who he says he is; no ordinary man has a sword like this. Look at the crest on it. The same mark is on the hunting horn. He is an impostor!'

Giselle stepped back in shock. What could this mean? Why was

Hilarion making such impossible accusations? What could cause him to invent such extraordinary lies? She stood shaking in disbelief.

But Hilarion persisted, too enraged to notice Giselle's distress. 'The sword, Giselle, the sword!' he shouted. 'Ask him about the sword!' He grabbed the hunting horn and blew long and loud. The hunting party would reveal the truth, he was certain of that.

Giselle moved hesitantly forward. 'Loys,' she asked in a trembling voice, 'is Hilarion right? Does this belong to you? What are you doing with a nobleman's sword?' Albrecht did not reply, and Giselle's heart fell. There *was* something wrong, then, but what? She turned away with a sob.

Just at that moment, the hunting party arrived in the village clearing, thinking that Bathilde must have called them back. Bathilde, hearing the confused noise, emerged from the cottage and stared, bewildered, at the scene before her. Who could have sounded the horn? And what on earth was *her* Albrecht doing here — and dressed in peasant clothes? The noble huntsman stood in disbelief at the sight of their noble companion. Suddenly all became clear. Horrified, Giselle realized that her Loys and Bathilde's Albrecht were one and the same person. She had been betrayed!

Stricken with grief, Giselle tore Bathilde's necklace off, and hurled it to the ground. Everyone stood in silence, touched beyond words

163

by her misery. Longing only for relief from the anguish in her heart, Giselle picked up Albrecht's discarded sword. She would kill herself! The horrified onlookers pulled the sword away. As if in a dream, Giselle began to dance again – the dance she had so delighted in with Loys just a short time ago. Her heart pounded, her vision blurred, her dance steps faltered. Swaying as if about to faint, she collapsed into her mother's arms.

Albrecht rushed forward but it

was too late. Giselle was dying: the shock had been too much for her weak heart. Smiling lovingly at Albrecht, she softly breathed his name and reached to touch his cheek. Even as she did so her hand faltered, and she fell back. Giselle was dead.

The mournful ghosts of young girls, who have been betrayed by their lovers and died before their wedding day, haunted the forest where Giselle lay buried. Any man who

crossed their path between moonrise
and sunrise was forced to dance
with them – to dance until he died.
This host of tormented ghosts was
known as the Wilis, and stories of
their dreadful power were whispered
in fear throughout the countryside.
No living man would freely choose
to visit the forest graveyard in the
Wilis's dark hours.

But late one night, Hilarion,
driven by his grief, set out to find
Giselle's grave. The graveyard
clearing was filled with an eerie

murmuring. Ghostly lights flickered and danced among the trees. The forester fled in panic, but the Wilis had sensed his presence, and began to gather.

As the moon rose, Myrtha, Queen of the Wilis, emerged to claim Giselle's soul. She summoned the spirits of the dead and they danced to her bidding: translucently beautiful in the moonlight, and terrifying in their pitiless obedience to their Queen. Their dance over, the Wilis turned to face Giselle's

grave. With a magic branch in her
hand the Queen of the Wilis bent
over the grave, murmuring a spell as
she did so.

The earth silently parted, and suddenly Giselle herself stood there, veiled in white, her arms crossed on her breast, as they had been in death. Moving as though asleep, Giselle glided forward, and stood motionless as the Queen lifted the veil that shrouded her lovely head. Following the Queen's commands in a mirror-like trance, Giselle began to dance. The young girl's innocent spirit spun round and round, rejoicing in her liberation from the cold grave.

As suddenly as they appeared
the Wilis disappeared into the trees.
They had sensed the arrival of a
stranger. The sad Albrecht had come
to lay white lilies beside Giselle's
grave. Hanging his head in remorse,
he remembered all that had been
light and life to him so short a time
ago.

There was a flicker of movement
against the trees. Giselle? Albrecht
shook his head in disbelief: surely
he must have been mistaken. But
no, there – again! It *was* Giselle!

170

Leaping to his feet, the Duke ran
to join the shadowy figure dancing
alluringly through the trees; she
disappeared again, only to reappear
behind him, and tap him softly
on the shoulder in silent greeting.
His heart leaped, and they danced
together as they had so often before.
And when the bewitched Giselle led
her lover deeper and deeper into the
forest, he willingly followed.

No sooner had the couple
disappeared than the Wilis swept
Hilarion back into the graveyard

clearing. Exhausted, he begged
for mercy, but none of the Wilis
could feel compassion: they had no
mercy to offer a man. They danced
relentlessly, enclosing Hilarion and
draining his strength still more.
Helpless and broken, the forester was
dragged inexorably to the lake. His
fate was sealed. The Wilis danced
in delight as he sank down into the
lake and drowned.

When Giselle and Albrecht
returned to the clearing there could
be no escape for Albrecht either: it

was his turn to die. Myrtha turned her cold gaze on him. Giselle's pleas were in vain: Albrecht must be danced to death.

Giselle's love for Albrecht, however, was as strong as the hatred that consumed the Wilis. Time and time again in the hours that followed she sought to save her lover. She was there, as lovely in spirit as she had been in life, offering Albrecht the strength he now so desperately needed. Each time he fell exhausted to the ground, Giselle ran forward to urge him to his feet again.

Eventually, Albrecht could stand no more. It was Giselle's fate to join the Wilis: it was Albrecht's fate to die at their hands. It seemed nothing could save them now.

But salvation was at hand, for the dancing and pleading had taken them through to dawn – and with the dawn light came the waning of the power of the Wilis. As a far-off rooster crowed, Albrecht fell, exhausted but safe, to the ground.

174

Giselle embraced him for one last
time. As the Wilis vanished like
mist back into the marshes from
which they had risen, Giselle's spirit
returned to the grave. Having saved
her lover, Giselle could now rest
in peace, no longer at the mercy
of Myrtha's power. And Albrecht
returned to the world, to live forever
more with the sadness of his lost
love.

Ballet Boots

Jan Burchett and Sara Vogler

'Saturday!' said Samantha Swan, the moment she opened her eyes. 'Ballet day!'

Sam loved Saturdays. Three hours of ballet and tap lessons to look forward to. And next Saturday was going to be the best ever. She

was going to dance a solo
called The Hummingbird
in an actual show! She
had a beautiful tutu to
wear, with shimmering blue
and green feathers. Miss Bussell, her
wonderful dance teacher, had got it
made specially.

Sam leaped out of bed and
pirouetted to the bathroom. She
dressed and then slid down the
banisters – toes pointed perfectly
– to have her breakfast.

'Ready for your lessons, Sam?'

asked her mother, buttering some toast.

'You bet, Mum!' beamed Sam. 'I can't wait!'

She happily munched her Sugarplum Flakes, being careful not to spill anything down her pink practice leotard.

The phone rang. Mum went off to answer it.

'Hello,' Sam heard her say in her best telephone voice. '. . . Yes, Sam Swan does live here . . . What? . . .

Really? . . . How fantastic! Sam will
be there! Goodbye.'

Mum rushed back into the
kitchen.

'That was Bog End Under-
Elevens Football Club,' she gasped.
'They say you're their new coach.
They're waiting for you to start
their training! How exciting!'

Sam dropped her spoon with
a splatter. 'I'm a ballerina, not
a football coach,' she exclaimed.
'Someone's made a mistake!'

Mum shook her head. 'They

179

definitely said Sam Swan. You can do it. You've got an hour before your first lesson.'

'You might like football,' whined Sam, 'but I hate it! It's muddy and dirty.'

'Bog End have chosen you,' said Mum. 'It's an honour.'

Sam thought about it. It didn't sound like an honour to her. It sounded like a nightmare. Then she heard Miss Bussell's voice in her head. 'If you've promised to appear, appear you must!' she'd declared when Maisie Green had tried to wriggle out of a ballet exam.

Sam's mum had said she'd be there. Sam had to go.

Bog End FC were the ugliest boys Sam had ever seen. They stared down at her, scowling and picking

their noses. They were covered in mud.

'You sure you're Sam Swan?' asked the goalie, scratching his head.

'Yes, I'm sure,' sighed Sam.

'You don't look like a football coach!' muttered a boy with a captain's armband. 'And we should know. We've had enough of them this year.'

'You phoned me,' insisted Sam.

The team started grumbling. Sam clapped her hands for silence.

Miss Bussell always did that and it always worked. It worked on the Bog Enders too. They quietened down and looked at her expectantly.

'Show me how you . . . erm . . . score goals,' she said.

'We've never scored a goal,' said the captain. 'Ever!'

'Our coaches always leave,' explained a boy in a bobble hat. 'They say we're useless cos we lose.'

'Brian's right,' said the goalie. 'And we've got a match against Marsh Road next Saturday

183

afternoon. We've got to
win or we'll be kicked
out of the league.'

'We realized we
needed a really good coach,'
Brian went on. 'My brother said
Sam Swan was the best coach there
was and my cousin's friend said
Sam Swan went to her school. So
I phoned you. Can you help us or
not?'

Sam was about to tell them they'd
got the wrong Sam Swan. Then
she looked at their miserable faces.

She couldn't say no — and anyway she wasn't a girl to turn down a challenge.

'Yes, I'll help you,' she declared. 'But first you must get fit.'

'Do we have to?' whined Brian, through a mouthful of crisps.

Sam gave him a Miss Bussell stare and he went red. 'Everyone on the pitch,' she said firmly. 'Marching on the spot. And call out your names so I know who you are.'

The team plodded in the mud and muttered their names in turn.

'Thank you. Now, arms in first position, please,' called Sam, showing them. 'And into second . . .'

The Bog Enders copied her and whacked each other in the ears.

'We'll do some "pliés" instead,' said Sam. She grasped the goalpost and bent her knees. 'They'll make your legs stronger, and strong legs score goals. Everyone line up at the fence.'

The team tried to do pliés and fell over like a row of dominoes.

Sam sighed. This was going to be hard work.

'Show me some tackling,' she told them.

She'd heard that was an important football skill. Freddie dribbled the ball slowly down the field. Colin took a swing at it and missed.

Sam felt like tearing her hair out – but as she had a beautiful French plait she decided not to. Besides, she knew what the problem was. Bog End had given up. Miss

Bussell wouldn't stand for that – and neither would Sam.

'What's your favourite thing in the whole world, Colin?' she asked.

'My hamster,' muttered Colin, embarrassed. 'She's called Giselle.'

'Pretend Freddie has stolen her,' said Sam. 'The only way to get her back is to tackle him for the ball – and tackle him hard!'

Colin's eyes lit up. 'I'll do it for Giselle!' he declared.

Freddie began his run again. Gritting his teeth, Colin charged up

188

and booted the ball right away. The
team cheered.

'Good work!' said Sam. 'Keep
practising. I have a ballet lesson
now. I'm rehearsing for an
important show next Saturday
evening. I'm going to dance The
Hummingbird. I'll see you here,
Monday, straight after school.'

'We don't train during
the week,' complained
Colin.

'You do now!' Sam
called over her shoulder, as

she ran off down the road to Miss Bussell's dance school.

On Monday after school, Sam went straight to the Bog End pitch. She taught the team some nifty tap-dancing steps. Now they could dribble the ball and dodge defenders at the same time.

On Tuesday she showed them how to do 'jetés' over the training cones. Now they could jump high enough to head the ball.

On Wednesday she taught them

how to do 'grands battements'
– with toes pointed as they swung
their legs. Now they were all
hammering the ball into the net.

On Thursday Robin the goalie
found he could leap between the
posts in a 'tour en l'air' with a
double twist. Nobody could get the
ball past him. And the defenders
learned a tap slide step and were
doing sliding tackles like experts.

By Friday the Bog Enders looked
like a different team – lean, mean
and very graceful in their boots.

'Well done, boys!' exclaimed Sam.
Miss Bussell always said praise
was very important.

'You're good enough to win.'

It was Saturday afternoon. Sam
stood on the touchline, wearing a
new orange-and-black striped tutu
– the Bog End colours. Giselle, the
team's new mascot, sat squeaking
with excitement in her orange-and-
black cage.

Sam gathered the team around
her.

'Go out to win, Bog End. And remember everything I've taught you.'

'Yes, coach!' chorused the team eagerly.

The match began. Colin kicked off. He passed to Brian. Brian put his feet in first position, trapped the ball and kicked it to Matt. The Marsh Roaders looked slow and clumsy as they tried to get possession. A defender came lumbering up but Matt performed a dazzling display of shuffle-step and

193

dodged him. He leaped towards
the goal. Sam was so delighted
she pirouetted around Giselle's
cage.

'Super play, Bog Enders!' she
called. But Matt stopped in his
tracks. Something was wrong.
Raucous laughter filled the air and
Sam realized that everyone was
making fun of her team – even their
own fans!

The Bog Enders stood and hung
their heads. All their clever moves
were being sneered at. Sam hadn't

told them this would happen!
Ashamed and embarrassed, they
went back to their old way of
playing. Sam screamed at them but
it was no use. By half-time Marsh
Road were four–nil up.

The Bog Enders sat in a sad
heap, too miserable even to eat their
oranges.

'We're going to be kicked out of
the league,' wailed Brian.

Sam stalked round them like the
bad fairy in *Sleeping Beauty*. 'Pull
yourselves together!' she exclaimed.

175

'You've forgotten every shim sham and "sauté" I taught you.'

'But they think we're stupid and girly!' sniffed Colin.

'They won't think you're stupid and girly if you score goals,' said Sam.

'But we're four–nil down,' mumbled Tom.

'That's because you decided to ignore your training.' Sam thumped her fist into her hand and looked sternly at each player. 'Today's the day Bog End do

something they've never done
before!' she declared.

The team sat up.

'Today's the day Bog End score
goals.'

The team sprang to their feet.

'Today's the day Bog End win!'

The team gave a great cheer.
They crossed hands and 'chasséd'
on to the pitch like the cygnets
from *Swan Lake*. Marsh Road were
so busy laughing at this graceful
entrance they didn't notice Colin
kicking off. They didn't see Terry

skipping down the right wing with the ball and passing it to Freddie. Freddie had all the time in the world to steady it. He paused in a graceful arabesque and then swung his leg through to hammer the ball at the net. The Bog Enders couldn't believe it! They'd scored their first ever goal! They skipped around the pitch with joy, Sam in the lead.

Marsh Road stopped laughing. They kicked off.

Tom did a perfect tap slide step to tackle and got the ball. He passed it

high to Colin who headed it
into the net with a soaring
jeté. Four–two!

Marsh Road didn't know how to
play against the Bog End Ballerinas.
They were fast, nimble and strong.
Before Marsh Road knew what was
happening, Simon and Matt had
both scored. The match was level
and it was nearly full-time.

The Marsh Roaders got in a
huddle. Sam could hear them
whispering and plotting something.
Then they took their positions on

the pitch. With confident looks on their faces, they kicked off. Their captain had the ball. Tom came forward in a series of jumps. The Marsh Road captain copied him. He wasn't very good but Tom was confused. He stopped.

'Take no notice!' yelled Sam. 'They can't do it – they haven't had the training. Just play as I taught you.'

But it was too late. The Marsh Road captain booted the ball to a huge midfielder who lobbed it down towards the goal. Their striker tried to jeté. It looked terrible but he made contact with the ball. It went storming towards the net. But Robin had been practising his tour en l'air. He flew across the goalmouth, did a double twist and caught the ball. Then with his arms in fifth position he threw the ball to Carl.

There was only a minute to go. Carl was confronted by a defender.

He did some heel-toe steps round the ball. The defender lunged at Carl. Carl sidestepped and passed to Jim. Jim chasséd with the ball and lobbed it on to Colin. Colin leaped with a super 'ballotté' and headed it on to Felix. Felix hammered the ball towards the net. Five–four to Bog End!

The referee blew his whistle. Sam screamed with delight and did six 'entrechats' in a row. Giselle squeaked with pride. Bog End had won their first ever match! She was about to run over to them when she suddenly remembered her show. There was no time to lose: she had a solo to dance.

Sam stood backstage. She heard 'Me and My Teddy Bear' burst from the piano as the three-year-olds began their dance. Butterflies were flapping around in her tummy. It was the most exciting feeling in the world. Pity she hadn't had time to say well done to the Bog Enders. It was the only thing spoiling a perfect day.

They'd probably find the real Sam Swan now and she'd never get to coach them again.

Sam got her glittery make-up done and her hair plaited to perfection. Her solo was in ten minutes. She went to the huge wardrobe where the costumes were kept. But as she turned the key, it broke in the lock! She rattled the doors till the whole wardrobe shook. It just wouldn't open. Her beautiful feathery costume was locked inside!

She heard Miss Bussell's voice.

'Sam to the wings. Hummingbird next.'

There was no time to get help.

Sam took several deep breaths. She couldn't let the audience down. There was only one thing for it – she would have to go on in her orange-and-black Bog End tutu, which was covered in mud from the pitch. But she couldn't dance The Hummingbird dressed like that. Whatever was she going to do?

Sam had promised to appear, so appear she must. Refusing to

panic, she walked gracefully on to the stage. She could see Miss Bussell watching from the other wing, looking stunned at the strange appearance of her star pupil.

Sam stared out at the audience. Then she heard cheering. It was the Bog Enders! All of them! They were waving their scarves and whistling. Sam held her head high and nodded at the pianist to begin. She knew what she had to do.

Sam danced the story of the Bog End victory. She whirled around the stage, dazzling the audience with her pirouettes, battements, entrechats and jetés. She danced the passes, the tackles, the headers and she danced every goal.

The audience stood and clapped and cheered. Sam thought they would never stop. Miss Bussell ran onstage and gave her a huge hug. Suddenly Sam felt herself being lifted up. She was on Colin's shoulders. The Bog Enders took her on a victory lap of the theatre!

Brian tugged on her tutu.

'My brother told me we'd got
the wrong Sam
Swan,' he shouted
up at her. 'No,
we haven't, I said.
We've got the best
football coach in the whole world.'

Sam beamed. 'Thanks, Brian. I'll
see you at training – Monday after
school. We've got matches to win!'

Nina Fairy Ballerina and the Magic Wish

Anna Wilson

Nina Dewdrop was in her bedroom at number five, The Chestnuts. Outside in the village of Little Frolic-by-the-Stream, sunlight was filtering through the horse-chestnut leaves, casting cool shadowy patterns across the woodland floor.

It was a perfect spring day, a day of fresh ideas and new possibilities. Nina gazed absent-mindedly at the shapes, while her little sister, Poppy, whizzed around the house with only one shoe on, shouting at Nina to help her find the other one.

'Oi! Neeny-Meany – have you taken my shoe? Where is it? You'd better not have thrown it out of the window . . .'

But even the irritating Poppy couldn't distract Nina from her thoughts today. It was Friday, and

that meant only one thing —
ballet!

Nina lived for her weekly ballet
lesson with Miss Thistle. It was
the only thing she enjoyed about
school. She had good friends, that
was true, but the time from Monday
morning to Friday lunchtime never
passed quickly enough. If Nina
wasn't dancing, or dreaming about
dancing, then she wasn't happy. It
was as simple as that.

The little fairy sighed contentedly
as she picked up her pink ballet

shoes and leotard and slipped them into her school bag. Then spreading her arms wide she skipped around the room, holding out her petal school skirt. She pirouetted and landed breathlessly in a heap on the bed.

'If I were a *real* fairy ballerina, I'd be able to pirouette without a wobble! *And* I'd have a proper ballet bag,' she said wistfully to herself. 'Oh, I WISH I could go to a ballet school and learn ballet every day!'

Poppy was hovering in the

212

doorway, still wearing only one shoe. '*I* wish you'd buzz off somewhere else too instead of moping around here whining about ballet the whole time,' she snorted contemptuously. 'But, before you go, will you PLEASE get your lazy wings whirring and FIND ME MY SHOE!' she shouted.

Nina stuck her tongue out at her sister and was about to retort that Poppy could buzz off herself, when:

WHOOSH!

A haze of lilac stars filled the

room. Nina jumped – she hadn't
said a magic spell, or waved her
wand. What was going on?

'Hello, Nina dear!'

The stars had faded to reveal a
motherly looking fairy with a kind
face. She was dressed in an old-
fashioned floor-length gown with a
high collar. Round her neck was
a string of tiny seed pearls, and her
immaculate white hair was done
up in a bun, held in place with
diamond pins and a sparkling
tiara.

'W-w-who are you?' Nina stammered.

Even Poppy was speechless.

The fairy smiled warmly. 'I am your fairy godmother, Heather Pimpernel,' she explained. 'Hasn't your mother told you about me?'

Nina hesitated, and Poppy blurted out, 'Oh, yeah! Don't you remember, Nina? Mum's always going on about our boring old fairy godmothers. I've always reckoned they must be a waste of time – they never remember our birthdays or anything—'

'Poppy!' Nina hissed, cutting her sister off before she could embarrass herself any further.

Heather raised her eyebrows at Poppy, but she was still smiling. 'I know; I haven't been around much – it's true. But you haven't needed me until now,' she said, looking pointedly at Nina.

Nina was puzzled. What was Heather talking about?

'You made a wish just now, Nina,' Heather prompted her gently. 'You said, "I wish I could go to a ballet school and learn ballet every day.'''

Nina blushed. 'I know,' she said. 'But I didn't think anything would happen. I mean, I didn't wave my wand or anything.'

Heather sat down in a comfortable armchair and said, 'You didn't need to, Nina. After all, as I said, I am your fairy godmother . . .'

Nina still looked confused, so Heather smiled and said, 'Let me explain. At your christening you received lots of lovely presents

217

from the guests, but I decided that
I would save my gift to you until
you were much older – until now,
in fact. As your fairy godmother, I
promised I would grant you a wish
– your heart's desire – once you had
reached an age when you would
use the wish responsibly, and not
just waste it on toys and sweets.'

Poppy guffawed. 'That's not
a waste. Hey, I wish for sweets,
Heather! Gimme some sweeties,
Heather!' she cried, fluttering around
the room.

218

'It's lucky I'm not *your* fairy godmother, isn't it, Poppy?' Heather teased. 'Don't worry, my dear, your time will come.'

Poppy curled her lip in a sneer, but stayed silent. She wasn't going to admit it, but she was every bit as curious as Nina to hear what Heather would say next.

'I think you are old enough now to use your wish, Nina,' Heather went on, 'but I want to be absolutely sure that you are wishing for the right thing.

Do you really want to go to ballet school?'

Nina nodded dumbly, her eyes shining. She was so overcome with the idea of her dream becoming reality that she could not think of anything to say.

Heather nodded too, but her face was more serious than Nina's. 'I see,' she said solemnly. 'And do you know what it would mean to leave your village school? There are no ballet schools near here. You would have to leave home to be a boarder,

so you would only see your mother
and sister in the holidays.'

At that moment, Nina couldn't
think of anything she would rather
do than leave Poppy behind in Little
Frolic-by-the-Stream. But then she
thought of her mother, and her best
friend, Blossom, and the sparkle in
her eyes died away.

Heather sighed. 'I thought so,'
she said. 'You haven't considered
this seriously enough. I'm not sure I
want to grant you this wish, Nina.
As well as leaving home, you will

221

have to work very hard indeed if
you want to be a ballerina—'

'Oh, but, Heather, I *do* want to
be a ballerina, more than anything
else in the whole of fairyland!' Nina
cried in earnest, flitting over to the
armchair. She stood before her fairy
godmother, a look of desperation on
her face, her hands clasped tightly
together.

'I'll tell you what,' said Heather.
'I will set you a challenge. If you
can prove to me that you are
serious about wanting to be a

ballerina, and that it is not just a passing fancy, then I will see what I can do.'

'Yes, yes!' Nina exclaimed. 'Anything!'

Heather laughed. Then she waved her wand and said:

'This dear little fairy god-daughter of mine
Has a heartfelt and burning ambition.
If I grant her this wish, then she'll be on cloud nine
Seeing all her dreams come to fruition . . .

223

But before I proceed, my Nina must see

That a ballet school needs to be certain

That she's up to the task so that one day she'll be

Centre stage, with a swish of the

curtain!'

A stream of lilac stars flowed out of
Heather's wand and landed softly
on Nina's head and shoulders. She
felt a shiver run through her, but
nothing else.

'I don't understand,' Nina said,
looking around. 'Nothing's changed.'

'Told you she was a waste of space,' muttered Poppy darkly.

Heather ignored her. 'You just get off to school now, dear,' she said to Nina, 'and whatever happens from now on, just remember: I'm on your side.' She winked mysteriously and, with a flick of her wand, she was gone.

Nina stood staring at the place where Heather had been moments before. She didn't know what to make of it all. Would Heather's spell help her or not?

225

But she had run out of time to think things over. Mrs Dewdrop was calling up to the two fairies to get a move on.

Nina picked up her school bag and called to Poppy to follow her downstairs to where their mother had found Poppy's missing shoe and was waiting to take them to school.

The morning lessons dragged by at an appallingly slow pace. At one point, Nina was convinced that the dandelion clock on the back

wall of the classroom had stopped
altogether. But at last the bluebell
rang for lunch, and it was time for
Nina's ballet lesson.

She fluttered as fast as her wings
would carry her to the changing
rooms and was ready in her ballet
things before Blossom had even
managed to open the changing-
room door.

'You could have waited for
me,' Blossom protested, huffing
and puffing as she struggled into
her violet leotard and shabby

227

yellow crossover. 'Why are you in such a hurry?' Blossom had never understood Nina's enthusiasm for ballet.

Nina just laughed nervously and, roughly shoving her hair into a ponytail, said, 'Sorry, but I've been so bored today, Bloss. I couldn't *wait* for this lesson.'

Blossom was sure there was more to it than that, but she was prevented from asking any more questions, as the ballet teacher, Miss Thistle, had arrived – and accompanying her was a very glamorous-looking stranger.

'Good afternoon, fairies!' trilled Miss Thistle, a delicate elderly fairy with grey curly hair. 'We are very honoured to have a special guest with us today: the renowned prima fairy ballerina, Ms Magnolia Valentine! Ms Valentine has for many years been a ballerina in the Royal Fairy Ballet, dancing the principal roles in *Giselle*, *Cinderella*, *The Nutcracker*, and many others. But the reason she is here today is

229

to fulfil another of her roles in the ballet world. Ms Valentine, perhaps you would care to explain?'

Magnolia Valentine curtsied graciously and studied the awestruck fairies before her. What a ramshackle bunch, she said to herself. Then her eyes settled on Nina, who was standing tall, her neck long and graceful, her hips turned out beautifully. Magnolia smiled.

Now *there* is a young fairy who stands out from the rest, she thought.

Aloud, she said, 'Good afternoon! I am here on behalf of the Royal Academy of Fairy Ballet in Oakton. I am on the board of trustees, and it is our job to travel fairyland, promoting the Academy. We are always on the lookout for new talent, and there is a scholarship awarded to the fairy who shows the most promise. I have come here today to see if any of you would like to attend an audition to win this scholarship. It is a great opportunity – many of fairyland's most celebrated ballerinas have benefited from the scholarship in the past – for example, Celandine Rosebud and of course the world-renowned Darling Bushel, who was herself headmistress of the Academy.'

Magnolia went on to tell spellbinding tales of her own time at the Academy and how it had led to a glamorous career, dancing all the principal roles for the princes and princesses of fairyland.

'I made friends for life at the Academy,' Magnolia murmured, gazing dreamily around the school hall. 'When you live and dance together like that, special bonds are formed that last forever.'

Nina felt a shiver go down her spine. This must be the challenge Heather had set her. She *had* to get that scholarship! She rushed to be the first to put her name on the audition list at the end of the lesson.

In the days and weeks that led up to the scholarship exam, Nina talked and dreamed of nothing but

233

ballet. She had been told that the examiners could ask her to perform anything that Miss Thistle had ever taught her, so she practised all five positions until she could even do them fluttering in mid-air. She also listened endlessly to the only ballet Daisy Disc she possessed, which was a recording of *Giselle*. She used it to work out a routine that would demonstrate the more difficult exercises Miss Thistle had shown her.

Poppy meanwhile was not

234

impressed. Every time Magnolia's name was mentioned in the Dewdrop household, Poppy would mutter, 'Magnolia Valentine? Magnolia Past-her-prime more like . . .' But secretly she was really worried that Nina would get the scholarship and that her wish to attend ballet school would be granted. However much she and Nina squabbled, Poppy knew she would miss her big sister.

The day of the examination arrived at last. Nina felt as though

235

a family of butterflies had taken up residence in her tummy, and she could not eat a crumb for breakfast. Her mother was very worried about her.

'Nina dear, you must eat something! Ballet is very physically demanding – you need to keep your strength up.'

But Nina was already grabbing her ballet bag and hovering in the doorway. 'Come on, Mum!' she cried. 'We'll be late for the audition!'

Magnolia Valentine was waiting in the school hall along with Miss Thistle and another fairy who looked very stern and scary, Nina thought. She was small and slender and her chestnut-coloured hair was scraped back from her face in a severe style. She wore tiny pince-nez on the end of her nose and peered over them as she addressed Nina.

'Good morning, Nina. I am Madame Dupré, the headmistress of the Royal Academy of Fairy Ballet. Ms Valentine and I will judge your audition today. Miss Thistle has explained what you have learned so far, and I would like you to demonstrate your knowledge of the five basic ballet positions. After that I will put on a piece of music, and you shall improvise a dance for us. When you are ready . . .'

Nina's legs felt so shaky, she did not think she could even manage to stand correctly, let alone improvise a whole dance. She sighed.

First things first, she said to herself, and carefully placed her feet in first position, her heels touching, her toes open, and held her arms 'bras bas' in a soft oval with her hands gracefully resting on the tops of her legs. Then, holding her breath, she pointed her right foot out to the side and placed it down on the floor again, at the same time moving her hands apart so that she was now in second position.

She moved on, through third and fourth position without a hitch. Then came fifth, which Nina always found the hardest. She knew that she needed to hold her turn-out perfectly for this position, as her feet should be parallel to each other, her left foot behind her right, the right heel touching the left toe, and the left heel tucked in tightly to meet the right toe. It was so difficult to hold this position without wobbling – and she had to hold her arms still too! It was at this point that Nina realized she hadn't been breathing deeply enough, and she started to feel dizzy. She lost her concentration and toppled over.

No one uttered a word, but Nina was sure she had ruined her chances of getting the scholarship.

So much for Heather being on my side, she thought bitterly, as she picked herself up off the floor, blinking back tears. *She could at least have come to support me. I don't believe she is going to grant my wish after all.*

Then, as Madame Dupré leaned over to a Daisy Disc player and put on a piece of music for the improvised dance, Nina caught a glimpse of a familiar tiara through the glass doors. Heather *was* there — in the corridor with Poppy and Nina's mum!

Right, thought Nina, a look of grim determination on her face. This is my last chance to prove to Heather how much I want this place at the Royal Academy.

She focused on taking some deep breaths to steady her nerves, and listened to the first few bars

242

of the music. It was *Giselle,* the

piece she had practised to! She

glanced across at Heather and saw

her fairy godmother wink at her.

Nina grinned, then curtsied to the

judges and began her routine. She

performed graceful

arabesques,

pirouetted

perfectly and

seemed to glide

across

the floor

like a swan on

243

clear water. As the piece drew to a
close, Nina curtsied again, pleased,
but not daring to meet the eyes of
her teacher or the two judges.

But Miss Thistle was already
clapping before the last note faded,
and Nina was sure she caught
the smallest flicker of a smile on
Madame Dupré's face. Magnolia
too was beaming at her.

It seemed she had made up for
her earlier wobble.

'Well done, Nina dear,' said
Magnolia. 'We will be discussing

244

your performance with our patron, Queen Camellia. Then, if you have been awarded the scholarship, you will receive notification in due course by grasshopper express. In the meantime, the best of luck to you, my dear. And keep dancing!'

As the next nervous fairy turned up to do her audition, Nina

245

fluttered excitedly out of the hall to meet Heather, Poppy and her mother.

'Did you see me?' she asked. 'Was it OK? I'm worried that I mucked up the exercises at the beginning, but they seemed to like my routine.'

Mrs Dewdrop was glowing with pride. 'Darling, you were wonderful!' she cried, hugging her daughter.

Heather had a satisfied smile on her face. 'You certainly have been

working hard, haven't you?'
she said.

Even Poppy was
impressed. 'Yeah, you
looked all right,' she said, giving her
sister a reluctant grin. 'But I'll miss
you when you go to the Academy,
you know,' she added quietly.

Nina sighed. 'I might not get in,'
she said. 'We'll have to wait and
see . . .'

But that's the thing about fairy
godmothers – they do have a habit

of making wishes come
true!

Nina Dewdrop, you have been
Specially chosen by our queen.
You passed your test with flying colours:
Your pirouettes surpassed all others.
So come, my dear delightful Nina,
And learn to be a ballerina!

I Don't Want to Dance

Bel Mooney

Kitty's cousin Melissa had started ballet classes.

'Why don't you go as well, dear?' suggested Kitty's mum.

'I don't want to dance!' growled Kitty, picking up her biro to draw a skull and crossbones on her hand. Mum sighed, looking at Kitty's tousled hair, dirty nails and the dungarees all covered in soil – from where Kitty had been playing Crawling Space Creatures with William next door.

'I think it would be nice for you,' she said, 'because you'd learn . . . you'd learn . . . Well, dancing makes you strong.'

'No,' said Kitty – and that was that.

But when Kitty's big brother Daniel came home from school and

250

heard about the plan, he laughed. 'Kitty go to ballet!' he screamed. 'That's a joke! She'd dance like a herd of elephants.'

Just then Dad came in, and smiled. 'Well, I think she'd dance like Muhammad Ali.'

'Who's he?' Kitty asked.

'He was a boxer,' grinned Dad.

That did it. If there was one thing Kitty hated it was being teased (although to tell the truth she didn't mind teasing other people!). 'Right! I'll show you!' she yelled.

So on Saturday afternoon Kitty
was waiting outside the hall with
the other girls (and two boys) from
the ballet class. Mum had taken her
shopping that morning, and Kitty
had chosen a black leotard, black
tights and black ballet shoes. Now
she saw that all other girls were in
pink. She felt like an ink blot.

Mum went off for coffee with
Auntie Susan, leaving Kitty with
Melissa and her friend, Emily. They
both had their hair done up in a
bun, and wore little short net skirts

over their leotards. They looked
Kitty up and down in a very
snooty way.

'You could never be a ballet
dancer, Kitty, cos you're too
clumsy,' said Melissa.

'And you're too small,' said Emily.

Kitty glared at them. 'I don't
want to dance anyway,' she said.
'I'm only coming to this boring old
class to please Mum.'

But she felt horrid inside, and
she wished – oh, how she wished
– she was playing in the garden

with William. Pirates. Explorers. Cowboys. Crawling Space Creatures. Those were the games they played and Kitty knew they suited her more than ballet class.

She put both hands up to her head and tore out the neat bunches Mum had insisted on. That's better – that's more like *me*, she thought.

Miss Francis, the ballet teacher, was very pretty and graceful, with long black hair in a knot on top of her head. She welcome Kitty and asked if she had done ballet before.

254

'No,' said Kitty in a small, sulky voice.

'Never mind,' said Miss Francis. 'You'll soon catch up with the others. Stand in front of me and watch my feet. Now, class, make rows . . . heels together . . . First position!'

Kitty put her heels together, and tried to put her feet in a straight line, like Miss Francis. But it was very hard. She bent her knees – that made it easier.

There was a giggle from behind.

255

'Look at Kitty,' whispered Emily.
'She looks like a duck!'

Miss Francis didn't hear. 'Good!'
she called. 'Now, do you all
remember the first position for your
arms? Let's see if we can put it all
together . . .'

Kitty looked at the girls each side of her, then at Miss Francis – and put her arms in the air. She stretched up, but was thinking so hard about her arms she forgot what her feet were doing. Then she thought about her feet, and forgot to look up at her arms.

There was an explosion of giggles from behind.

'Kitty looks like a tree in a storm,' whispered Melissa.

'Or like a drowning duck!' said Emily.

'Shh, girls!' called Miss Francis
with a frown.

And so it went on. Kitty struggled
to copy all the positions, but she
was always a little bit behind.
Once, when Miss Francis went over
to speak to the lady playing the
piano, she turned round quickly and
stuck her tongue out at Melissa and
Emily.

Of course, that only made them
giggle more. And some of the
children joined in. It wasn't that
they wanted to be mean to Kitty

– not really. It was just that she looked so funny, with her terrible frown, and her hair sticking out all over the place. And they thought she felt she was better than all of them. But of course the truth was that the horrible feeling inside Kitty was growing so fast she was afraid it would burst out of her eyes.

Everybody seemed so clever and skilful – except her.

I *am* an ink blot, she thought miserably.

It so happened that Miss Francis

259

was much more than pretty and graceful; she was a very good teacher. She saw Kitty's face and heard the giggles, and knew exactly what was going on. So she clapped her hands and told all the children to sit in a circle.

'Now, we're going to do some free dancing,' she said, 'so I want some ideas from you all. What could we all be . . . ?'

Lots of hands shot up, because the class enjoyed this. 'Let's do a flower dance,' called Melissa.

260

'Birds,' suggested Emily.

'Let's pretend we're trees . . . and the hurricane comes,' called out one of the boys.

'I want to be a flower,' Melissa insisted.

Miss Francis looked at Kitty. 'What about you? You haven't said anything,' she said with a smile.

Kitty shook her head.

'Come on, Kitty. I know you must have an idea. Tell me what we can be when we dance. Just say whatever comes into your head.'

'Crawling Space Creatures,' said Kitty.

The children began to laugh. But Miss Francis held up her hand. 'What a good idea! Tell us a little bit about them first, so we can imagine them . . .'

'Well, me and William play it in the garden, and we live on this planet, which is all covered with jungle and we're horrible-looking things, with no legs, just tentacles like octopuses. And so we move about by crawling, but since we

like the food that grows at the top
of the bushes we sometimes have
to rear up, and that's very hard,
see. And we have to be careful, cos
there's these birds that eat us if they
see us, so we have to keep down.
Sometimes William is the birds, and
tries to get me . . .'

'All right, children – you're all
Crawling Space Creatures. We'll see
if we can get some spooky, space-
like music on the piano . . .'

The lady playing the piano smiled
and nodded.

So they began. Most of the children loved the idea, but Melissa and Emily and two other girls looked very cross and bored.

'Down on the floor, girls!' called Miss Francis.

Kitty had a wonderful time. She listened to the music and imagined the strange planet, and twisted her body into all sorts of fantastic shapes. After a few minutes Miss Francis told the others to stop. 'All watch Kitty!' she said.

So the children made a circle, and Kitty did her own dance. She lay on the floor and twisted and turned, waving her arms in time to the music. Sometimes she would crouch, then rear up, as if reaching for strange fruit, only to duck down in terror, waving her 'tentacles', as the savage birds wheeled overhead . . .

At last the music stopped, and all the children clapped. Kitty looked up shyly. She had forgotten where she was. She had lost herself in her dance.

When the lesson was over, Miss Francis beckoned Kitty to come over to the piano. None of the children noticed; they were all crowding round the door to meet their mothers.

'Now, Kitty,' said Miss Francis quietly, 'what do you think you've learned about ballet today?'

'It's hard,' said Kitty.

'Well, yes, it is hard. But what

else? What about your space dance?'

'That was fun!'

'Because it was *you*?'

Kitty nodded.

'Well, we'll do lots of made-up dances too, and you'll find you can be lots of things — if you let yourself. That's what modern ballet is all about, you know. Now take this book, and look at the pictures, and you can practise all the positions for next week . . . You are coming next week?'

Kitty nodded happily, and went off to find Mum. Outside in the hall Melissa and Emily glared at her.

'Look at my tights – they're all dirty,' moaned Melissa.

'All that crawling about on the floor – so babyish!' said Emily, in the snootiest voice.

'If you knew anything, you'd know that's what modern ballet is all about,' said Kitty, in her most wise and grown-up voice. 'I shall have to teach you some more about it next week. Now, if you'll just let me past, I'm going to go home and practise.'

Practice Makes Perfect

Vic Parker

Hannah Hermione Henrietta Bogg was the last child in a family of seven boys. First there was Alfie, then came Ben, Callum, Daniel, Elliot, Frank, Gabriel and – just when her mum and dad had given up all hope of ever having a baby girl – Hannah had finally arrived.

When it came to looking after their rather large family, Mr and Mrs Bogg weren't short of love, care or patience. However, they *were* very short of cash. Which meant that everyone was squashed together in a teeny tiny house. There was a teeny tiny kitchen, which they couldn't all fit into at the same time. Everyone had to take their turn at the teeny tiny kitchen table to eat their meals. There was a teeny tiny

living room with a teeny tiny telly.
Everyone had to take their turn on
the teeny tiny sofa to watch their
favourite programmes. There was a
teeny tiny bathroom with a teeny
tiny bath, a teeny tiny sink and
a teeny tiny toilet. Everyone was
allowed five minutes to get ready
in the mornings and there was an
egg timer stuck on the wall, which
buzzed to tell you when your time
was up! Last of all, there were just
two teeny tiny bedrooms. Mr and
Mrs Bogg squashed into the teeniest

tiniest bedroom. The seven boys squashed into the other teeny tiny bedroom. Which meant that there wasn't a bedroom at all for poor Hannah once she'd grown out of the cot that had been crammed into her parents' room.

Still, Hannah didn't whinge or whine. Mr and Mrs Bogg had cleared out the cupboard under the stairs and squeezed a teeny tiny mattress in there. It may not have been a proper room, but it was Hannah's very own private space.

At least she didn't have to share
with her smelly brothers – and she
had better things to do than listen
to them chatter on about football.
After school she liked to sneak
into her cupboard, shut the door,
lie on her mattress and gaze up
at the poster she had stuck on the
slanted ceiling. The poster was of
the world-famous Russian ballet
star, Sasha Sparklikova, wearing
a dazzling-white tutu, a dazzling-
white tiara and a dazzling-white
smile, balancing on the very tiptoes

of one foot as though she
was an angel about to fly
away on her dazzling-
white wings.

Hannah thought that Sasha
Sparklikova was the most beautiful,
most glamorous, most amazing
person in the whole world. Hannah
had only ever seen ballet on the
telly — she knew that there was no
way Mr and Mrs Bogg could ever
afford to take her to the theatre
to see a real live performance,
so she never dreamed of asking.

But every now and then, after waiting for Alfie, Ben, Callum, Daniel, Elliot, Frank and Gabriel to finish watching alien shows and basketball games and cowboy films and disaster movies and Emergency Hospital and football matches and Ghost Hunters . . . and whatever else they wanted to see on the teeny tiny TV, Hannah managed to catch bits and pieces of her favourite ballerina's performances in *Swan Lake*, *Coppélia*, *Cinderella* and *Sleeping Beauty*. And when

Sasha Sparklikova danced, it took Hannah's breath away. There was nothing she wanted more than to dance like Sasha. Back in her cupboard, Hannah would shut her eyes tight, hum a few bars of music and imagine she was performing on stage, carried away somewhere magical by the music – an enchanted woodland glade! – then coming back down to earth and curtsying graciously to the audience as they roared their applause and threw a carpet of flowers at her

277

perfectly pointed feet. But Hannah was always strict to remind herself that this could only ever be a wonderful dream . . .

. . . Until the morning of her eighth birthday arrived. Now the Bogg children weren't like other children, who got up on their birthdays to find a heap of presents from their parents, and money from grannies and grandpas, and gift vouchers from aunties and uncles, and then a mountain of cards and presents from stacks of friends

invited to a party with a magician
and a disco and sandwiches and
sweets and crisps and Coke and an
enormous cake and jelly and ice
cream and going-home bags packed
with goodies at the end of it all. Oh
no. The Bogg boys and girl were
used to finding one present on the
breakfast table – just one, a joint
gift from everybody – wrapped up
in last year's paper. As Hannah
squeezed into the kitchen that
morning she wondered what her
present might be, before realizing

there wasn't the usual box waiting
for her on the breakfast table. Not
a bag. Not an envelope. Not even
a party popper, hiding behind the
cornflakes. Still, Hannah knew how
hard up her parents were and she
was determined not to show her
disappointment. She put on her
best, brightest smile and made up
her mind to pretend that she'd quite
forgotten it was her special
day at all.

But suddenly Mr and Mrs
Bogg appeared in the doorway.

'Happy birthday, darling,' they said, knocking their elbows against the walls as they gave Hannah a huge hug. Then her seven brothers took it in turns to squeeze in and out of the teeny tiny kitchen to do the same. 'You didn't think we hadn't got you a present, did you?' Mrs Bogg went on, and Hannah's heart began to race. 'It's just that this year we've scrimped and saved for something that we can't wrap up. You know how your father and I often do extra shifts at the chicken-pie

factory so that Alfie can do his
athletics, Ben can do his basketball,
Callum can do his karate, Daniel
can do his drumming, Elliot can do
his electric guitar, Frank can do his
football and Gabriel can do his go-
karting?'

'Yes . . .' breathed Hannah, not
quite sure where this was going.

'Well . . .' announced Mr Bogg,
with a nervous smile, 'for your
birthday present, we thought you
might like . . . ballet lessons.'

'B-b-ballet lessons!' stammered

Hannah and promptly burst into tears with the emotion of it all.

'Don't get upset, darling,' said Mrs Bogg. 'You can always do something else instead. We just thought that you'd quite like the chance to be like Sasha Sparklikova but perhaps you'd prefer yoga?'

'Ballet will be wonderful, thank you,' said Hannah, pulling herself together with a wobbly smile. 'When can I start?'

★

That Saturday
morning, Mrs
Bogg took
Hannah down to
the church hall on
the high street to Miss
Avril's Adagio Academy
of Dance. Hannah had
never been so nervous, especially
when she said goodbye to her mum
and walked through the door to
find herself in a room full of little
girls — and two little boys — all
dressed neatly in proper ballet kit.

Hannah looked down at herself in dismay. She was wearing Gabriel's old PE plimsolls, some of Frank's faded ankle socks, a pair of Elliot's outgrown shorts, and a T-shirt that once belonged to Daniel, with a worn-out tracksuit of Callum's over the top of everything.

She glanced enviously at a miniature ballerina preening herself in the corner of the room. She had golden hair swept back under a pink headband into a perfect bun with a pink ribbon around it,

285

stray curls held in place with pink sparkly slides. She was wearing a pink leotard with pink tights, a pink crossover cardigan, a short pink floaty skirt, and pink satin shoes with pink shiny ribbons. At her feet lay a pair of pink leg warmers, a pink quilted outdoor coat with pink fur around the hood and a pink shoe bag with *Cordelia Carruthers-Bumstead* embroidered on it in sparkly pink thread. As Cordelia caught sight of Hannah, she began to snigger. 'Whatever do you look like!' she sneered. 'You do know that this is a ballet class and not a rugby match?'

At this, Hannah felt herself turn pink — well, red — from head to toe. She was just about to turn and escape back through the door when Miss Avril came over and took her hand. 'You must be Hannah,' she smiled, leading her gracefully into the centre of the room. She turned to the other children and announced, 'Positions, please, everyone!' Then a hunched little old lady bundled up in a woolly coat and hat started to tinkle away at the piano, and the ballet class began . . .

Afterwards, Hannah floated home with her feet hardly touching the ground. Her head was filled with the positions she had learned: special knee bends called 'pliés', gentle springs called 'sautés' and flowing arm movements called 'port-de-bras'.

The week before her next lesson dragged and DRAGGED and *DRAGGED* but Saturday finally arrived, and when Hannah arrived at the Academy Miss Avril had a fantastic surprise waiting for her. 'I've had a rummage through the lost property box,' she said, her eyes twinkling, 'Try these on for size.' She handed Hannah a black leotard and little black skirt, a black headband and – best of all – a pair of black ballet slippers. Hannah didn't care that they were old and worn and shabby. They were her very own ballet shoes!

289

She hurried off straight away to
get changed. As she wriggled into
the clothes, one precious item at
a time, she felt herself transform
from Hannah Hermione Henrietta
Bogg – scruffy second-hand girl
– into Hannah Hermione Henrietta
Boggoffski – Russian ballet star
extraordinaire!

Hannah walked into the class with
her head held high. She was sure she
already looked more elegant, more
graceful, more poised . . . But as she
pointed her toes she heard Cordelia

Carruthers-Bumstead sneer at the top of her voice, 'Ooooh, look at her – Hand-Me-Down Hannah! The prima ballerina of lost property! She's even got someone's old shoes on – look, they've got *SS* written on the bottoms!'

Hannah stopped in shock. A shiver ran down her spine. *SS?* She knew those initials! She lifted up her foot and, sure enough, there on the sole of the tatty ballet shoe, someone had written *SS* in black biro. 'How fantastic!' she gasped.

Cordelia Carruthers-Bumstead snorted. 'What on earth do you mean, how fantastic?'

'Well, think about it – SS. Maybe these shoes once belonged to Sasha Sparklikova herself!' Hannah murmured, her eyes widening. 'She might have worn these to practise in when she was a little girl. She might have worn these when she got top marks in her first exam. She might have worn these when she auditioned for her place at the Russian ballet school! I'd much rather have Sasha Sparklikova's tatty old shoes than some boring new ones.'

As Hannah skipped off, she felt her toes tingling strangely. Meanwhile, Cordelia Carruthers-Bumstead glowered and pouted, kicking the wall with her perfect pink slippers. Sasha Sparklikova's shoes! she thought. Why can't I have them? I want them! And her eyes narrowed to mean little slits as she watched Hannah begin to warm up . . .

★

As the weeks went by, Hannah practised and practised her ballet wherever she could. She didn't care who saw her or how silly she looked as she 'jetéd' along the pavement on the way to school, pirouetted in the playground or trembled on one toe in the teeny tiny garden at home. Every Saturday, the children in the ballet class noticed how Hannah was getting better and better and better. Soon her toes were pointier, her legs stretchier, her arms floatier,

294

and her leaps lighter than anyone else's.

How on earth can she have got that good that fast? Cordelia Carruthers-Bumstead wondered irritably to herself, as she stumbled over her 'pas de chat'. I bet it's those shoes. I bet they really are Sasha Sparklikova's! I bet they've got some sort of magic in them. I'm sure that without Sasha Sparklikova's special shoes Hand-Me-Down Hannah would be rubbish!

Eventually, after weeks of

preparation, the day came when the pupils of Miss Avril's Adagio Academy of Dance were to take their ballet exams. It was a terrible crush in the church hall changing room as everyone squeezed in to get ready. It was so cramped that Emily Earnshaw and Ashia Patel put a leg each into the same leotard! Hannah didn't mind the squash, as she was used to being jogged and jostled by her brothers in their teeny tiny home. So she didn't complain when Cordelia

Carruthers-Bumstead bumped into her and knocked over her ballet bag (which was really Ben's old sports bag), spilling her things all over the floor. 'So sorry, Bogg,' smirked Cordelia. 'What a shame you're now going to look dirty as well as shabby in the exam! Let me help you pick everything up . . .' Cordelia trampled on Hannah's clothes, crumpled them up into a ball, thrust them at her and walked away chuckling.

Hannah hurriedly got dressed and

looked around for her ballet shoes.
They weren't in her bag. They
weren't on the bench behind her.
They hadn't been flung into the
corners of the changing room. 'My
shoes!' Hannah wailed in horror.
'I can't find my shoes! What am I
going to do?'

'Oh dear,' sighed Miss Avril,
rushing over at the commotion.
'There's no time to do
anything about it now
– your exam's about
to begin. I'll have to

298

ask the examiner if you can dance in your old plimsolls. Quickly now, come with me!'

Trying hard not to panic, Hannah followed Miss Avril and the other girls into the exam room. As she waited for Miss Avril to have a quiet word with the examiner, she saw Cordelia Carruthers-Bumstead with a smug look on her face, looking like the cat who got the cream. Cordelia's mean green eyes flicked down towards the floor – and as Hannah followed her gaze

she saw that on Cordelia's pinkly
perfect feet were Hannah's shabby
ballet shoes!

Hannah couldn't believe it.
Her eyes were as wide as saucers.
Cordelia must have deliberately
knocked over her bag so she
could pinch her lucky shoes! But
as Hannah's heart thumped and
bumped inside her chest, she thought
she heard Sasha Sparklikova's voice
in her head saying, 'Darleenk, you
do not need my shoes – you can
dance the beeyootiful ballet without

them . . .' And before Hannah had time to wonder about how strange this was, the exam began.

As it turned out, everything that could possibly go wrong went wrong that day for Cordelia Carruthers-Bumstead.

As Cordelia lifted her arms over her head in her port-de-bras there was a loud P-I-N-G! The elastic in her ballet skirt snapped and it fell off in wrinkles round her feet. As she bent her knees in a plié there was a

mighty R-I-P! and a big split
appeared in the seat of her leotard.
As she lifted her leg and pointed her
toes, she suddenly got a tremendous
urge to sneeze. 'A-A-T-I-S-H-O-O!'
she exploded, drenching the
examiner. Finally, as she leaped
around the room, she tripped over
her feet, tumbled across the floor
and ended up flat on her face with
her bottom in the air. How the
examiner tutted and shook her head!

Meanwhile, Hannah did her best
not to be put off by her lack of

ballet shoes or by Cordelia's dancing disasters. She took a deep breath and tried to imagine she was Sasha Sparklikova herself. She concentrated so hard on everything she had practised that she quite forgot she was in the draughty old church hall – she danced as magically as if she was on a big stage in front of a proper audience.

And when the examination was over, Hannah was overjoyed to be told that she had passed with top marks. Cordelia, on the other

hand, had failed miserably. 'Take
your stupid shoes!' the nasty girl
screamed, ripping them off her feet
and throwing them at Hannah.
'I never really believed they were
Sasha Sparklikova's anyway!' And
she stormed off, away from Miss
Avril's Adagio Academy of Dance,
never to dance another 'petit-jeté' as
long as she lived.

And that is why Hannah
Hermione Henrietta Bogg grew
up to be a famous ballet star, with
her name in lights outside theatres

all over the world, and with enough money to buy her family a massive mansion with three rooms per person, and why Cordelia Carruthers-Bumstead grew up to be a stable-girl, mucking out pony poo all day long.

(Hannah never did find out whether her shoes had once

belonged to Sasha Sparklikova.
Once she had outgrown them, she
put them back into Miss Avril's
lost property box, and saved up
enough money to buy her own pair.
But a few years later, another girl
beginning at Miss Avril's Adagio
Academy of Dance borrowed the
shabby old pair of shoes with *SS* on
the bottoms. And as she nervously
took her place at the barre she was
sure she could feel a strange tingle
in her toes . . .

Swan Lake

Belinda Hollyer

Prince Siegfried had been looking
forward to his twenty-first birthday
celebrations for months and now,
at last, they had begun.
He and his friends had
been invited to attend
some entertainments

just outside the palace grounds,
devised by local villagers.

The villagers were waiting
excitedly when the palace party
arrived. Some of the young girls
gave flowers to Siegfried and others
helped to fix the maypole in place,
while Siegfried smiled his thanks and
offered drinks to everyone. Then
the dancing began, with group after
group eager to show what they
had prepared for the royal party.
Siegfried and his friends enjoyed
themselves enormously. His old

tutor and one or two of his friends
had rather too much to drink, and
when Siegfried's mother arrived it
reminded her of what she must say
to her son.

'Now that you have come of
age,' she said firmly, 'I expect you
to take life a little more seriously.
You must find a suitable bride:
the future Queen.' Siegfried tried
to make light of it, for he had no
desire to marry — but his mother
persisted.

'At the ball tomorrow night,'

she reminded him, 'will be the six most eligible young women in the kingdom. All you have to do is choose one of them to be your bride.' And then, with a further icy glance of disapproval at the drinkers, Siegfried's mother swept back into the palace grounds.

The villagers were still dancing, but Siegfried's good humour had disappeared. He hated the idea of an arranged marriage and his mother's determination made him uneasy. His friends tried to distract

310

him, but although he rejoined the celebrations the young Prince's unhappiness persisted.

By now, dusk had fallen. His friend Benno glanced up at the evening sky and saw a flight of swans passing overhead on their way to the forest, their great wings beating in unison. 'Look!' he shouted. 'Let's get together a hunting party and follow those swans!'

Siegfried's spirits were immediately raised, and the young men, armed with crossbows, hurried off after the swans.

The great lake shimmered in the moonlight, unruffled by even the faintest breeze. A ruined chapel stood on the shore, from which an evil spirit in the form of a great owl surveyed its dominions. Hearing the hunting party, it

slunk back to hide in the depths of
its lair.

Siegfried's friends had run ahead
of him, and continued along the
side of the lake. As soon as they left
the clearing, Siegfried arrived – and,
with a rush of wings, so did the
swans.

Excited, Siegfried knelt beside
the lake, his crossbow at the ready.
As he watched, one of the swans
alighted on the ground beside the
ruined chapel. It seemed not to be
a swan at all. Was it a woman or

313

a bird who stood
there, with such
fragile grace
and beauty?
A woman
surely, for
her slender body
was that of a
young girl – but the beautiful face
was framed by swan feathers, and her
pale dress was soft with swansdown.
As Siegfried watched, the wondrous
creature bent her head so that her
cheek touched her shoulder, just as

a swan might preen its feathers. The
moonlight, breaking through the
clouds, glittered on a delicate lacy
crown nestled in her hair.

Siegfried advanced softly, but his
movement caught her eye, and she
froze with shock. Her body quivered
in terror and her arms beat the
air frantically like a swan's wings.
The hunter begged her not to fly
away, but the swan-woman looked
at the crossbow that he still held.
Shuddering with fear, she asked if
he intended to kill her.

Already in love, Siegfried swore
that he would never dream of
harming her, he implored her to
stay and talk to him. Accepting the
Prince's word, the beautiful swan-
woman agreed.

Her name, she explained, was
Odette, Queen of the Swans. She
had not always been a Swan
Queen, but had been bewitched
by an evil spirit. All her mother's
tears, which now filled the lake
before them, had not moved the evil
spirit to compassion. His magic had

condemned Odette to be a swan, except between midnight and dawn, when she was permitted to regain her human form. The swans who flew with her were swan maidens too, under the same extraordinary enchantment. And a swan she would always be – unless a man swore to love her, married her and never loved another. Then she would be released from the swan-magic forever.

'I will release you from this evil spell,' declared Siegfried, 'for I will

317

always love you. I will marry you, and never love another. Dearest Odette, come away with me now!'

Just at that moment the evil spirit emerged, sensing a threat to his wicked enchantments. His owl face was beaked and dangerous, and his talon-like hands stretched out to Odette, ordering her to return to his side. With a defiant shout, Siegfried lunged for his crossbow. Standing tall in the moonlight, fearless in his anger, Siegfried took careful aim. Let the evil spirit die at his hand!

But Odette ran to put herself between the crossbow's aim and the owl-sorcerer's menacing figure. 'If you kill him, I too will die! Only after the spell is broken will I be safe from harm.'

Siegfried lowered his crossbow; the sorcerer vanished, and Odette fell thankfully into her lover's arms. 'Come to the palace tomorrow night, for my birthday ball,' begged the Prince. 'I am supposed to choose a bride – and I will choose you, in front of all the world.'

But Odette was too frightened of the sorcerer's powers. 'If I tried,' she murmured, 'he would stop at nothing to spoil your plans and make you break your promise, Siegfried. Then I will be a swan forever!'

As they talked, another danger threatened – for Siegfried's hunting companions had discovered Odette's swan-maidens, and in the soft moonlight thought they had tracked down the swans they intended to kill. Odette ran to safeguard them.

If they tried to kill her maidens, they would have to kill her first! When Siegfried explained, the huntsmen suddenly saw the swan-maidens more clearly, and bowed humbly before the lovely creatures.

As the first streaks of dawn approached the shore, Odette had no choice but to return to the lake with her swan-maidens. She held out her arms longingly to Siegfried, but her feet carried her irresistibly back to the lake, where the swans waited beating their wings, and

the cruel-beaked owl hovered,
reclaiming his victims.

The next night, the palace was
filled with glittering excitement and
glamorous figures — for everyone
of any importance in the kingdom
had gathered to celebrate Prince
Siegfried's birthday. What a party it
was to be!

Siegfried, however, found it hard
to attend to what was happening,
and impossible to enjoy himself.
All he could think of was the night

before, and his meeting with the beautiful Swan Queen. How he longed to be at her side, rather than at his party! Try as he might to be polite to his guests, his thoughts kept returning to the lakeside, and to Odette and her maidens.

Cross that her son should seem so distracted and inattentive, Siegfried's mother drew his attention to the six beautiful Princesses just entering the room. They bowed gracefully to the Prince and his mother, and then danced a stately waltz together.

Siegfried descended from his throne to the ballroom floor as though he were in a dream. Solemnly, he took the hand of each of the six Princesses in turn, and led her in a dance while the whole room watched, eager to see which of the six he would choose. 'How strange!' the courtiers murmured to each other as they watched: the Prince didn't seem interested in any of the Princesses. Although he was courteous to each, none seemed to warrant a second glance from him.

324

What on earth could be wrong?
Was he ill?

The Prince's mother grew angry
with embarrassment. She thanked
the bewildered young Princesses
for their elegant dance and
congratulated them on their beauty,
doing her best to smooth over the
awkward situation. Then she turned
to her son. 'Which one will you
choose?' she demanded. The room
grew quiet in anticipation.

'These Princesses are indeed
lovely,' replied Siegfried coldly to

his mother, 'but I will marry none
of them, Mother, for I love another.
I will marry no one but her!' And,
bowing low to the Princesses, he
turned to gaze out of the window,
his thoughts lost in the night.

A trumpet blast broke the
scandalized silence. A herald ran
in and conferred with the Prince's
mother, for an unknown couple had
arrived and, although he didn't have
their names on his guest list, they
seemed very grand. Should he allow
them entry? Impatiently, the Queen

326

agreed: any distraction would be welcome at this stage.

To a crash of cymbals and a flickering of the lights the doors few open and the strange couple entered the room. The man was a tall, bearded knight who called himself Von Rotbart. He introduced his daughter, Odile, to Siegfried and his mother, bowing low before he glanced up and fixed the Prince with strangely glittering eyes.

The Prince was beside himself with excitement. Looking at Odile,

327

he thought he saw his heart's desire, his beloved Odette. He did not see that the coldly beautiful woman who stood haughtily in front of him was returning his passionate gaze with icy calculation. For Odile was the sorcerer's daughter, and Von Rotbart was the sorcerer himself. He had bewitched Siegfried, so that the Prince saw and believed only what the evil spirit wanted him to, and nothing else.

The real Odette beat her arm-wings against the great windows of

the ballroom – but in vain.

Siegfried was spellbound.

He rose from his throne, descended

the steps and stood before Odile. As

he looked deep into her cold black

eyes, the vision of Odette drew back

from the window, exhausted. Only

a single swan's feather remained

for a moment, and then sank like a

breath of air to the ground.

Siegfried escorted Odile into

the garden, gazing at her with

delight: his Swan Princess at his

side, and all was well. Now the evil

Von Rotbart turned his charm on Siegfried's mother, and she, beguiled by his magic, invited him to sit by her side. Who was this man? Could his daughter be a suitable match for her son? Really, she must find out more . . .

The entertainment began again, with renewed energy. Everything was sparkle and delight again, and when Von Rotbart suggested that Siegfried and Odile might dance together, Siegfried's mother graciously agreed.

Siegfried danced as if in a dream.
Dazzled by his love, he did not see
the real Odette had returned to
the ballroom window once more.
Odette knew that if the evil spirit
could trick Siegfried into betraying
her – to say that he loved Odile
and would marry her – then the
Prince would have broken his
promise to her, and she would be
a swan forever. She beat against
the window with a feathery arms,
crying in a silent agony of despair.

Her movements caught Von

331

Rotbart's eye. He moved between the window and the Prince, smiling as he did so. With Odile's claw-like hand in his, Siegfried led her across the room to her father.

'I want to marry your daughter,' he said to Von Rotbart. And wondered why the room had gone dark, just for a heartbeat.

Von Rotbart smiled his assent, and turned to Siegfried's mother: she smiled her assent in return. But Von Rotbart needed to be quite, quite sure he had won.

'Will you love my daughter forever? Swear you will!' he demanded, watching the Prince closely through narrowed eyes. 'Swear you will never love another!'

Siegfried blinked to steady his head; he felt a confused echo of another time, another promise. But when he looked at Odile, his head cleared miraculously. Of course, that was why he had heard the echo of his promise. His beloved was by his side!

'I swear it!' he cried into the

333

darkening echo of the room, as
with a shriek of triumph, the spirit
revealed himself and his daughter
as their true selves. In a moment,
Siegfried realized what he had
done, and turning away in horror
he finally saw Odette fluttering
hopelessly at the window. He rushed
from the ballroom with a cry of
grief, but Odette had vanished.
The Prince ran through the dark
forest to the lake, fighting against
a gathering storm, hoping against
hope that he could find Odette

again, and somehow put right the terrible wrong he had done.

The swan-maidens had gathered at the lake to comfort their grief-stricken Queen. 'I have been betrayed,' she sobbed, 'and so I must be a swan forever; forever in his power. The evil spirit has won.' But the swans urged her to wait for Siegfried's arrival.

'You know it wasn't his fault,' they pleaded. 'How could a human have withstood the evil spirit's

335

enchantment? How could Siegfried have known he was under a spell?'

Frantic with sorrow, the Prince staggered into the clearing. He searched in growing panic amongst the maidens. Their compassion finally overcame them, and they parted to reveal Odette hidden amongst them.

Siegfried begged Odette for her forgiveness, and out of love she gave it to him, weeping for their lost life together. Only death could free her now from the owl-spirit's power.

With a crash of thunder, the
evil spirit appeared, exulting in
his triumph. He taunted Siegfried
with the reminder that he had
sworn to marry Odile, and of the
consequences of his promise. At his
command, the swan-maidens danced
in the moonlight, unable to resist or
to deny his will.

Odette knew that she must die.
With a last loving embrace, she left
Siegfried's side and ran towards the
lake, to throw herself into its depths.
And Siegfried, unable to imagine life

without his beloved Odette, realized that he, too, must join her.

Thunder and lightning ripped through the sky as the evil spirit tried to stop the lovers, for he knew that his power would be destroyed by their death: his evil could not withstand such perfect love. But he could not stop them. As they sank beneath the waves, cradled in each other's arms, the evil spirit crumpled to the ground, an empty bundle of feathers. His evil reign was over.

The swan-maidens watched from

338

the shore as Odette and Siegfried
sailed away to another world.
Nothing could separate them now;
never again would unhappiness
touch the beautiful Queen and her
loving Prince.

Acknowledgements

The compiler and publishers wish to thank the following for permission to use copyright material:

Ian Billings for 'Bunty's Dream' by permission of the author; **Jan Burchett and Sara Vogler** for 'Ballet Boots' by permission of The Agency (Ltd) London on behalf of the authors; **Julia Donaldson** for 'The Magic Shoes', first published in *Princess Mirror-Belle and the Magic Shoes* by Julia Donaldon (Macmillan Children's Books, 2005), by permission of the Caroline Sheldon Agency on behalf of the author; **Fiona Dunbar** for 'The Mice of Maison Zobrinska' by permission of The Agency (Ltd) London on behalf of the author; **Belinda Hollyer** for 'Giselle' and 'Swan Lake', both stories first published in *Stories from the Classical Ballet* by Belinda Hollyer (Macmillan Children's Books, 1995), by permission of David Higham Associates on behalf of the author; **Geraldine McCaughrean** for 'The Nutcracker', from *The Orchard Book of Stories from The Ballet* by Geraldine McCaughrean, first published in the UK 1994 by Orchard Books, a division of The Watts Publishing Group Ltd, 338 Euston Road, London NW1 3BH; **Bel Mooney** for 'I Don't Want to Dance!', first published in *Darcey Bussell: Favourite Ballet Stories* (Bodley Head, 2001), by permission of David Higham Associates on behalf of the author; **Vic Parker** for 'Practice Makes Perfect' by permission of the author; **Anna Wilson** for 'Nina Fairy Ballerina and the Magic Wish' by permission of The Agency (Ltd) London on behalf of the author.

Fairy Stories

Chosen by Anna Wilson

Every fairy has a story to tell.

Be spirited away to fairyland, and visit
the wonderful worlds of dream fairies, funny
fairy godmothers, a sweet-toothed cake
fairy and a fairy who learns a lot
about friendship.

This magical story collection is a
must for all fairy fans.

Princess Stories

Chosen by Anna Wilson

**Every princess
has a story
to tell.**

A pretty-perfect princess and a badly behaved
princess, a princess in love and a princess
in BIG trouble . . .

These are just a few of the princesses on
parade in this fun, magical story collection.

A selected list of titles available from Macmillan Children's Books

The prices shown below are correct at the time of going to press. However, Macmillan Publishers reserves the right to show new retail prices on covers, which may differ from those previously advertised.

Fairy Stories	978-0-330-43823-0	£4.99
Princess Stories	978-0-330-43797-4	£4.99
Mermaid Stories	978-0-330-45406-5	£4.99
Christmas Stories	978-0-330-44600-6	£4.99
Pirate Stories	978-0-330-45148-2	£4.99

By Anna Wilson

Puppy Love	978-0-330-45289-2	£4.99
Pup Idol	978-0-330-45290-8	£4.99
Puppy Power	978-0-330-45291-5	£4.99
Kitten Kaboodle	978-0-330-50771-4	£4.99

All Pan Macmillan titles can be ordered from our website, www.panmacmillan.com, or from your local bookshop and are also available by post from:

Bookpost, PO Box 29, Douglas, Isle of Man IM99 1BQ

Credit cards accepted. For details:
Telephone: 01624 677237
Fax: 01624 670923
Email: bookshop@enterprise.net
www.bookpost.co.uk

Free postage and packing in the United Kingdom